THE ANGEL AND THE RING

Sigmund Brouwer

HARVEST HOUSE PUBLISHERS

EUGENE, OREGON

Cover by Left Coast Design, Portland, Oregon

Cover image © Cecil G. Rice

THE ANGEL AND THE RING
Copyright © 2005 by Sigmund Brouwer
Published by Harvest House Publishers
Eugene, Oregon 97402
www.harvesthousepublishers.com
ISBN 0-7369-0294-5

Library of Congress Cataloging-in-Publication Data

Brouwer, Sigmund, 1959–
   The angel and the ring / Sigmund Brouwer.
     p. cm. — (The guardian angel)
   Summary: In 1364, orphaned Brin, raised by gypsies and watched over by a guardian angel, must decide who to trust with the medallion left to him by his parents and which has a mysterious connection to the city of Rome and to the Holy Grail.
   ISBN 0-7369-0294-5 (pbk.)
   [1. Guardian angels—Fiction. 2. Grail—Fiction. 3. Rome (Italy)—History—476-1420—Fiction. 4. Romanies—Fiction. 5. Angels—Fiction. 6. Christian life—Fiction.] I. Title.
   PZ7.B79984Aml 2005
   [Fic]—dc22
                                         2004016247

Printed in the United States of America

06 07 08 09 10 11 12 / BC-MS / 10 9 8 7 6 5 4 3

With Love to Savannah,
you'll always be an angel to me...

It wasn't easy to put this story about a boy named Brin into words. Not that I'm complaining. Angels never complain.

You humans, on the other hand, are so childlike that your constant whining to God often tempts me to roll my eyeballs in disgust. Yet I don't. First, angels don't even have eyeballs to roll. Second, rolling eyeballs is a silent way of complaining, and, for those of you who weren't paying attention, I've just made it clear that angels don't complain.

So, telling you it wasn't easy to write this story is simply an observation. *Not* a complaint. If you decide that my observation sounds like a complaint, it's your fault, not mine.

Writing isn't easy for many humans either, from what I can tell. But let me stress that it seems infinitely slower and more cumbersome for an angel. (Cumbersome. *Kum-burr-sum*. If you watch too much television, you may have difficulty with the size of this cumbersome word. *Kum-burr-sum*. It means bulky, awkward to handle, a big load.)

See, if you were another angel, we would just have a meeting of minds, so to speak. In an instant, you'd know everything I wanted you to know. Neither of us would have to say a single word, let alone write it out.

Not that I'm complaining.

At this point, I expect you are curious about how this meeting of minds works between one angel and another.

Good. Curiosity is one of the *nice* childlike things about you humans. But don't expect me to give you the answer. Nor am I going to answer exactly why and how I've written down this entire story about Brin. There are many questions that won't get answered for you until you are on the other side of life. Deal with it.

If you continue with me, however, I promise to answer a lot of *other* questions by the end of this book. You will have to pay attention, though. Otherwise, don't waste your time reading more. There's always television. Or nose picking, which is at least useful and has the same entertainment value. Especially to angels, who may be invisible and watching when you least expect it. (Enough said about that.)

Have I established, then, that it has taken a lot of effort for me to put this story into your words and that you will get answers worth learning? Good. Show your gratitude and stay with me.

Even though I won't promise a happy ending.

What, you say, not fair? Who says it's supposed to be fair? When I'm sent from heaven as a guardian, I sure don't get that promise. I've seen it end happy for the ones I'm sent to guard. I've seen it end sad.

That might sound mean and horrible, but it's not.

Whatever happens to the people I'm watching over—happy or sad—works to the greater good of those who believe in our Father and His love. Think of His work as a beautiful painting. When I'm stuck in a particular place and time on earth to watch over someone, I see only what you see: individual brushstrokes. The little bits and pieces that make up the painting. I trust all of those brushstrokes will make sense when our Father has finished the entire painting, though. You should too. Life will be easier on you that way.

As for a happy or not-so-happy ending for each person under my watch, learn and remember an important concept. Maybe the most important concept. Ready?

You humans are given the freedom to make choices.

Yes. Choices. You are responsible for what you do. Don't blame other people. Especially don't blame me or other angels.

Choices.

Imagine you're in a room with a screwdriver in your hand. You have a choice. Jam it into a nearby electrical outlet? Or not? You may think that's an obviously easy choice. But in guarding different people through centuries of your human history, I've seen a lot of things that, in comparison, make jamming a screwdriver in an electrical outlet look like a smart thing to do.

Take the people of a small mountain village one sunny morning in Italy.

At the time, my assigned charge was a boy named Brin. Probably not a great name, but that's the way it goes.

Brin was a gypsy. Sixteen years old. I'd been watching over him for years by then. Standard stuff, like keeping him from crawling into open fires when older gypsies in the camp forgot to pay attention. Or when he was older, standing between him and wolves when he wandered into the forest. Nothing really exciting enough to pass on to other angels.

I'm not suggesting, though, that his childhood had been easy.

He'd been born before the invention of the telescope. Before steam engines. Before trains or train tracks. Before ouchless bandages, cough syrup, and flu vaccination shots. Yes, even before the invention of the remote control.

This part of Brin's life took place in AD. 1364 (That means *Anno Domini*. Latin for "the year of our Lord." At least you humans have had enough sense to keep track of time from the birth of Jesus, the Son of our Father.)

Brin lived when wealthy people often wore flea traps under their clothing. That's what I said. Flea traps. Little cages filled with a piece of fat to attract fleas so the fleas would get stuck in the trap and not be all over a person's body.

The 1300s were not pleasant, as you can see. Fleas, lice. No soap, no showers, no toothpaste. But try not to think about that and concentrate on the important parts of the story.

Like how humans in Europe had just spent centuries of short life spans and miserable living conditions because of all the knowledge that had been lost after the fall of the Roman Empire.

Like how the people of that small village that morning in the northern part of Italy were all about to make a choice.

Based on greed.

I was there to watch it all. I was there especially to watch Brin. I knew him well enough by then that I could guess his thoughts just by reading his face.

And let me say that the morning did not turn out the way either of us expected.

1

"Dare to wager a gypsy?"

Brin had heard Marcel issue this challenge dozens of times, in dozens of crowds of peasants, in dozens of market towns. It was like casting fish bait.

"Spawn of the devil!" an old woman cried out. "Thieves! No good layabouts! Get back on the road!"

Brin had heard this before too. He stood among perhaps 20 people. There were housewives, farmers, apprentices, maids, and beggars.

Marcel held a piece of rope above his head. The rest of the rope was wrapped around Marcel's thick body, coiled over one shoulder and under the opposite armpit.

"One end of this rope, there!" Marcel pointed to the tiled roof of an ancient stone building. He moved his arm to point across the cobbled street. "The other end, there! And I walk across!"

Marcel paused. His black eyes glittered in the midafternoon sun.

Brin wished he could have the same arrogant manner. Brin wished he had the same dark good looks, the same heavily muscled body. At 21, Marcel was in his prime.

Brin? Brin was small. Fair-haired. He rarely spoke above a whisper. No amount of wishing could give him the same power and command that Marcel held among the gypsies.

There too was the matter of Brin's entrance into the gypsy world. His mother, a gypsy princess, had died from the Black Death barely a day after giving birth to Brin. This ill omen had cast a dark shadow on Brin. Another baby might have received sympathy for entering such a harsh world without a mother.

Not Brin.

His father had not been a gypsy, and those from outside the clan were hated and distrusted. But it didn't stop there. Brin's father had done far worse than most strangers. He had taken the gypsy princess away and had married her in a church. Nearly a year later, she had returned without Brin's father, ready to give birth and in the final stages of the dreaded plague.

This was all Brin knew about his parents. Neither had been around to care for him. Both had left Brin an inheritance of disgrace, something Brin paid for dearly among his gypsy clan daily.

"I shall walk across this rope!" Marcel repeated. He stood on top of a wagon, and no one nearby could fail to notice him or his family members sitting on the wagon behind him. "And I shall be blindfolded!"

More peasants, farmers, and idle townspeople gathered. It was a hot day. Brin smelled bodies that had not been washed for months, waste thrown from houses onto the cobblestones, and manure from cattle driven down the streets.

Brin took refuge in his mind by thinking of cool nights in the gypsy camp. He thought of his quiet world in the shadows, outside the circles of gypsies who sat around the campfires, and how those moments seemed to bring him what little sanctuary he could ever find in a day.

"Yes, blindfolded!" Marcel said. "I will juggle three eggs as I walk from one side to the other!"

"What is your wager?" someone finally called from the crowd.

Despite his lonely thoughts, Brin smiled. There was always one person to ask that simple question. And so the hook was set.

"Why, if I drop one," Marcel said, "every person gathered to watch will collect ten lira."

The noise of the growing crowd swelled into excited babble.

"Quiet! Quiet!" a man shouted.

Brin stood on his tiptoes to see above the shoulders of the people around him and caught a glimpse of this new speaker. He was a large man with a red face beneath a dark beard, wearing the luxurious colors of a wealthy shopkeeper. A circle of hair ringed his bald head.

The crowd obeyed his command. This man, Brin decided, was one of the town's respected leaders. Perhaps a mayor.

"If you drop an egg," the man said, "you will pay ten lira to every person gathered."

"That is so," Marcel said.

"Blindfolded, walking across a rope, juggling three eggs."

Marcel smiled. "If you like, have men beneath with pitchforks pointed upward at me. So if I fall, I impale myself."

Crowd noise began to rise.

The shopkeeper raised his hands to keep the noise down.

"You announced this as a wager," the shopkeeper said. "Not a contest. What, then, is the wager?"

Marcel waited until every eye in the crowd was upon him. It grew so quiet that the only sounds were of squawking chickens in the market stalls further down the road.

"What, then, is the wager?" Marcel said. "The only fair wager possible."

Again, he paused.

Brin admired Marcel's showmanship. Marcel knew how to play a crowd.

"If I succeed," Marcel said. "Each of you gathered pays me ten lira."

People in the crowd turned to each other to trade their views on this.

Marcel did not ask for silence. Instead, he held up a small leather pouch, bulging with coins. Heads turned back to him. Mouths shut.

"Is ten lira not a fair price to pay for entertainment? After all, I risk not only my hard-earned coins but my very life!"

Brin knew with certainty that the wager would occur.

Few were the opportunities for entertainment. These were not men and women of royalty, able to hire musicians, throw extravagant feasts, or travel with bodyguards to summer estates near the sea. Instead, these simpler poor folk lived their entire lives within the town walls, or on farms within a half day's walk from the town. A hanging in the public square was entertainment for them. Or drunken brawls. Or the spectacle of chasing gypsies.

They would take the wager, simply for the chance to watch someone risk falling onto pitchforks.

Brin knew, too, what was going through the minds of most of these townspeople.

Greed.

The townspeople hated the gypsies. *If he drops an egg,* Brin knew they were thinking, *we will make him pay. If he succeeds, we will not pay, but run him and his clan out of this town. After all, they are only gypsies.*

"I will take that wager," said the wealthy shopkeeper with a greedy smirk. "Any others?"

All in the crowd raised their hands and voices.

"So be it!" the shopkeeper shouted to be heard above them. "Prepare the rope."

2

In the half hour it took Marcel to secure the rope from roof to roof, the crowd beneath tripled, buzzing with excitement.

On the wagon nearby, the gypsy families watched in silence. Other members of the clan sold simple wooden toys from a makeshift stall in the market. And the remaining gypsies were back in camp, in a field some half mile from the town.

Brin was the only gypsy not in the company of others. He was accustomed to this. He was also accustomed to wearing drab rags while all the other gypsies wore brightly patterned shirts and silky pants. Among them all, he was like a little brown sparrow hopping out of the way of larger, prettier birds.

And among the crowd gathered in the market square, Brin was just another poor peasant, of little worth and far beneath anyone's notice.

Which is why the gypsy clan kept Brin in drab rags. With his dirty blond hair and paler skin, no one would ever think Brin was a gypsy. Nor would anyone treat him with the suspicion accorded to all gypsies. This sparrowlike appearance made Brin very valuable to his clan.

Finally, Marcel was ready. He stood on the edge of one roof and bowed to the entire crowd.

The wealthy shopkeeper had arranged for large men to stand beneath the rope, armed with pitchforks. Perhaps he only wanted men ready to get the payment when Marcel failed. Or perhaps he truly wanted Marcel impaled at the slightest misstep. It was hard to say. Such was the life of a gypsy.

"There are now many more of us!" the shopkeeper shouted upward. "You will still pay each of us ten lira?"

"Most certainly," Marcel said, teeth gleaming in a wolflike grin. "As you will all pay me if I succeed?"

"Yes, yes," the shopkeeper said impatiently. "Begin."

With a flourish, Marcel pulled out a thin, dark strip of cloth. He tied it over his eyes and behind his head. Brin doubted any in the crowd could see what Brin knew. Marcel had positioned the blindfold over his nose in such a way that he could easily peer downward.

Marcel held out three eggs in one hand.

He took his first step onto the rope. It sagged slightly but held his weight.

"Juggle!" someone shouted. "Juggle!"

Marcel tossed the first egg in the air. Then the second. Then the third. Without walking ahead, he juggled them in perfect rotation until he was comfortable with the rhythm.

Brin had seen Marcel keep six eggs in the air. This was nothing for him.

The crowd, of course, did not know this. They watched in total concentration as Marcel finally took another step on the rope. And another.

Before Marcel was a quarter of the way across, the crowd began to shout and jeer. They did not want to see him complete the balancing act.

The men below began to jab their pitchforks upward. And the jeering grew louder.

Brin had no doubt Marcel would succeed. But Brin did not pause to admire Marcel's great athletic ability.

No, the jeering of the crowd meant Brin, too, must begin his task.

He moved beside a farmer whom he had spotted earlier. This farmer had a small leather bag hanging at his waist from a strap at his shoulders. Brin slipped his hand into the bag and withdrew half the coins inside. He knew that to remove all the coins might lighten the bag too much.

As Brin moved on, he tucked the stolen coins inside a leather bag inside his own shirt.

He eased himself through the pressing crowd, stepping close to a housewife he had noticed. She, too, had a purse easily plucked.

Brin kept moving through the crowd, picking the pockets of victim after victim. It was simple. All attention was on Marcel. People jostled each other in close quarters. Brin had deft quick hands, capable of stealing under far trickier conditions. Here, with the noise and the bumping, it was impossible to detect his actions.

In the center of the rope, Marcel paused. He pretended to sway dangerously. He almost dropped an egg.

It was intentional, of course. All of this had been set up to allow Brin to pickpocket these simple people. Marcel simply wanted to give Brin as much time and opportunity to continue taking coins from unguarded purses.

Marcel resumed his balancing act, getting closer and closer to the other roof, juggling as he walked.

Brin slipped out of the crowd, toward a crooked side street. This was the time he must make his escape.

Marcel hopped onto the far roof, pocketed the eggs, and untied the blindfold. Already, the crowd was beginning to leave. Brin went with the stream of people, slipping away with a half dozen men and boys.

"What is this?" Marcel shouted with pretended outrage. "You wagered and lost fairly! Come back! Come back!"

"Gypsy fool," the wealthy shopkeeper replied. "How do you propose to force payment?"

The men with pitchforks ringed the shopkeeper and looked purposefully upward at Marcel. It was a show of force that made anything Marcel might say seem totally hollow.

"This is not fair!" Marcel cried. "I might have been killed. Had I dropped an egg, I most surely would have been forced to pay my end of the wager."

"Shut your mouth and be grateful we let you live," the shopkeeper said. "As it is, you have outworn your welcome. You and your families move on before we take action upon you."

Brin did not hear the end of the conversation. Nor did he need to. It always played out the same way. They were only gypsies, after all. No citizenship. No homes. No protection. Spat upon. Feared as messengers of black magic. And used by parents to frighten children. *Behave,* mothers would cluck, *or gypsies will steal you in the night to take you to faraway lands.*

Brin walked slowly, careful to press his arms into the heavy, newly-filled pouch resting against his stomach. It would do no good to allow a jangle of coins. It would do no good to drop the pouch and spill coins across the road. If that happened and some peasants reached for their own pouches to make certain their own coins were safe...

Pickpockets were sometimes hung without trial. Brin knew that.

Each time he and Marcel played this game, Brin fought the sour fear in his stomach. All it would take was a single mistake and...

A hand grabbed Brin's shoulder.

"Come with me," came the low voice.

Brin spun around to see a man wearing a hooded cloak. Shadows cast his entire face into darkness.

"Let go of my shoulder," Brin said. The sourness in his stomach grew heavier. "I have no business with you."

"I think you do," the hooded figure said. "Or shall I raise a public outcry and be declared a hero for catching the lad who boldly robbed the crowd?"

3

Brin hesitated. He quickly decided he could outrun this man. And if not outrun, at least dodge him. More than once Brin had darted away from pursuers, his life depending on his fleetness and agility.

Yet if the man cried for help and the entire town gave chase, could Brin escape? The streets ahead were narrow and crooked, a double-edged sword. As easily as these streets gave him the opportunity to spin and twist away, they could also run him into a dead-end alley. This town, as with all towns, was strange to Brin.

The hand upon his shoulder dropped away.

"Run, if you think it will help you," the hooded man whispered. "But I will find you later as effortlessly as I found you now."

Stragglers passed them by, uncaring of the conversation of strangers.

"What is it you seek?" Brin asked.

The man in the cloak laughed. "I could just as well ask that of you. What is it you seek?"

Brin clutched his arms tighter to himself, feeling the edges of the stolen coins against his belly. He wanted to use this conversation to give him time to allow his wits to find a way of escape. "What would any man seek but wealth and ease of living?"

The hooded man laughed again. "You answer my question with a question. Any man might seek wealth and ease of living, but you have not declared that as your own dream. Are you any man? Is wealth and ease of living what you seek?"

"And you," Brin said, "also answered my question with a question. What is it you seek?"

"Well spoken," the man said. "I can see your father in you. I want to help you. Now answer my question. What do you seek? What do you dream of?"

My father in me? Brin felt as if his heart had been prodded with a hot iron. *This man knew my father?*

"My dreams," Brin said, keeping his face still despite the swirling questions inside him, "are my own matters. Not to be shared with a stranger who does not even show his own face."

"I will answer, then, at the proper time," he said. "Perhaps tonight, when we meet at the north bridge along the stream, when the town bells ring midnight."

"How do I know this is not some sort of trap?" Raised as a gypsy, Brin had been taught to keep eternal suspicion.

"If it is harm I want to bring on you," the man said, "all I need to do is call and you will be taken away for stealing from the pockets of the townspeople."

The man shrugged, which moved the hood slightly. Brin saw, or thought he saw, a reddish-blond beard.

"Besides," the stranger said, dropping his shrug, "what could you, a poor gypsy boy, have of value to steal? Tonight, you shall see that it is an offer of help that I bring."

"Why are you so certain I will appear?" Brin asked, although already he knew he would go as asked. *If this man knew my father...*

"Your curiosity will drive you to it. You wonder how it is I knew you picked the pockets of these townspeople. You wonder why I do not call for your arrest. You wonder about your father. And you wonder what it is that I will offer as help."

"Perhaps," Brin said coolly.

"As you say." The hooded man's voice was low. And amused. "Until then, ponder my question. What is it you seek?"

~ Angel Blog ~

Brin didn't know it, of course, but he had never really been in danger from the hooded man—or from the crowd—with me nearby. And the hooded man wasn't another angel, in case you're wondering.

Had the hooded man tried to harm Brin, I would have stopped him. Now don't ask me how I knew that was what our holy Father wanted me to do. It's impossible to explain. The closest you would understand is a form of instinct, but even that is a bad explanation. All I can tell you is that at that moment, I *knew* Brin was to be protected in the crowd—even though I can't tell you why he was supposed to be protected. Not even angels know what is in the mind of our holy Father.

As for protecting him, angels have many different methods. You'd never suspect most of them as belonging to an angel. Gust of wind, maybe. A tree falling across a road to keep a driver from the next corner where a bridge is out. A barking dog that causes you to take a different path. That sort of thing.

If you want to read some classic examples, go to the Bible. I wish I could tell you I was one of the angels in the lions' den with Daniel, but others were sent that time. Believe me, we all heard plenty about it from those angels later. You know, like sometimes when your friend gets back from a really fun vacation and goes on and on about all the details.

Anyway, there was a lot I could do to protect Brin. But there were some things I couldn't do, and here's where you should probably learn more about what angels can and can't do.

23

We can't create. That's something only our Father can do. Let me just say, if you could have been there at the beginning, the *very* beginning, you would be the biggest believer in the universe. Yes, *that* beginning. Of time. Of the universe. Not that I was there. But the great thing about the spiritual world is that time and space don't form a prison for us like they do for you. (Believe me, you'll find out someday. On the other side. By then, you'll be glad you trusted in our Father.)

As I was saying, since time and space don't bind us, we angels have a good idea of what it was like at the beginning of creation. "Spectacular" doesn't give it justice. It's beyond comprehension. Then again, if you television watchers got off the couch and walked through the woods and took a close look at our Father's handiwork every once in a while, you might get an inkling of how incredible it was.

What else can't angels do?

Angels can't change substances. Again, only our Father can do that. So don't come to me and ask for that lump of lead to be changed into gold. I'm not a fairy godmother. And yes, I've had that request before.

Angels can't alter the laws of nature. Again, only our Father can.

Same thing goes for miracles. Angels can't perform them. Only our Father can.

And here's something that might surprise you. Angels can't see into your heart. (After centuries and centuries of experience with you humans, however, we can make some pretty good guesses.) Some of you wise guys might be saying, hey, no problem, any good doctor can get a good view of the human heart. But that's not the heart I'm talking about—and you know it.

Angels can't change your hearts either. Remember that thing called "choice"?

Anyway, that's a lot of what we can't do.

It's good to keep all that in mind because the fallen angels can't do any of it either. Fallen angels. That would be Satan and his gang. They can't do any of our Father's special stuff either. No creating, no changing of substances, no altering the laws of nature. No searching or changing the hearts of people.

Why's that important to remember?

Too many humans worry about demons because they believe demons have special power. Not so. Good thing, because I have plenty of stories about their bad intentions and how we'd been sent in by our Father to protect you against them. Nasty bunch, those guys. Of course, they've known for a long time that when they picked sides, they picked a loser—Satan himself. For eternity. That would make anyone bitter.

I know, I know. What about Brin?

He meets a hooded stranger. The hooded stranger seems to know a lot about him. The hooded stranger throws out the bait: *I'll tell you about your father.*

No surprise that Brin is about to take that bait like a skinny trout dying from starvation.

Hey, I was as curious as Brin about his father and his whole mysterious childhood. (Did I forget to mention the strange ring he wears on a leather strap around his neck, the only thing his parents had left him? I think I did! Well, now you know.) In other words, I sure hoped Brin was going to decide to meet the stranger on the bridge that night.

I also had a good idea I was finally about to find out why I'd been sent to watch over him. I'd been with him for years already, and now it seemed very likely that this was the point in his life where I would really be needed, the point in his life that he and I would both learn what path our Father hoped he would take.

Only if he made the right choice..

4

Gypsies were never welcome near towns. To return to camp, Brin had to walk a mile into the countryside with the heat of the sun on his back. As he arrived at the gypsy camp, he noted with surprise that he did not remember a single step of his journey through the fields and over stone fences.

The stranger knew my father!

Brin barely noticed the familiar setting in front of him. Although the countryside changed week by week as they moved from place to place, the gypsies always set their tents up in the same manner—an inner circle and an outer circle. Everything looked the same—wagons that carried their belongings from town to town, wooden posts driven into the ground to tie goats, mules hobbled and grazing in a grassy area beyond the camp, iron pots hanging over the grey, dead ashes made by the nightly fires.

The stranger had known my father!

Unconsciously, Brin let his fingers play lightly with a small ring hanging from a leather strap around his neck. His father had given it to his gypsy princess mother in his dying moments. She, in turn, had left it for Brin. It was the only possession that linked Brin to his long-dead parents.

The stranger had known my father!

How many nights had Brin fallen asleep wondering the simplest things about his father? Where had he come from? Where had he been going? What kind of man had he been?

Not one of the elder gypsies ever spoke of Brin's father or mother, and Brin had learned very young not to ask. His questions were answered with dark looks at best and with blows to the head at worst.

Brin had decided his father must have been handsome and dashing, perhaps even rich. How else could an outsider have stolen the heart of a gypsy woman?

Brin had decided their love must have been of the power and strength to match any heroic song. Why else had his mother chosen his father over her own people? Why else had his father risked his life to take her away? Growing up, Brin had seen how fiercely the gypsy men protected their women from outsiders, even to the point of execution. How much more they would have fought to keep a gypsy princess among the clan, he figured.

The stranger had known my father!

Brin was so deep in thought and hope that he failed to hear footsteps behind him. His first warning of trouble was the stinging whack of a branch rod against his back.

"Lazy idler!" came the screech.

Brin spun around. His first reaction was anger at himself for stupidly allowing this to happen.

His attacker was the old great-grandmother of the clan. She was tiny and always wore a long black dress, her toothless face little more than a lump of puckered flesh. During the day, she wandered the camp, muttering curses at imagined enemies. At night, she squatted in a hunch over a tiny fire, rocking back and forth on her heels as she sang tuneless songs.

"Bring her back," the old woman wailed. She swung the branch at Brin. He jumped out of her reach easily. "She belongs with us!"

The crazy old woman believed it was Brin, and not his father, who had taken away her gypsy princess granddaughter. As often as she could, she would pounce on Brin and attack him with the same demands.

"Bring her back!" she wailed again.

Brin never lost his temper at the old woman's meanness. He felt sorry for her and her poor, confused mind.

"She belongs with me..." her voice trailed off pitifully.

What pain she must bear, Brin thought. *She believes my mother is still alive. She's looking for someone who is never going to return.*

As she took another swing at him with the switch, Brin jumped away. He dug into the pouch of coins beneath his shirt and offered her one, choosing not to speak.

"Bribery!" she screeched. "You cannot buy her from us!"

She took the coin anyway, holding it in the sunlight to examine the silver. With her attention off him, Brin took slow, careful steps as he backed away from her. Rarely did he run from one of her attacks, although he could have left her and her tottering steps far behind. The few times he had escaped her that way, her wailing and screeching rose as if he were striking her. And with her bad eyesight, there was too good a chance she might fall and break her fragile bones if she chased him. Better to stay and take her abuse, Brin reasoned, so that she wouldn't hurt herself.

Brin eased back further while she examined the coin. The best way to leave her was to distract her and then quietly sneak away to...

A large hand grabbed the back of Brin's neck.

"So, you worthless dog, are you giving away my coins?"

5

Brin didn't have to turn around to know who held him. And this time he would suffer more punishment than a whack from a stick carried by an old woman.

"Give me the pouch," his attacker demanded.

It was Marcel's father—Antonio—a large man with red eyes and broken veins on his nose. Marcel's father spent most of his nights drinking sour wine. During the day, he had a constant headache, and his temper reflected it.

Antonio cuffed Brin with his free hand. "Give me the pouch," he repeated.

Brin was again angry at himself for getting caught. As he reached for the coins, though, he didn't allow himself to whimper. He never did. Not around Marcel. Not around

Antonio. Not around any of the gypsies. He had stopped crying long ago.

Antonio took the pouch with a surly grunt. He held the pouch between his teeth and, with both hands, shook Brin, listening for the jingle of any coins hidden in Brin's clothes. Then he patted Brin to make the search complete. Antonio's hand stopped at the ring around Brin's neck for a moment, and then moved on. Everyone in the camp knew about Brin's keepsake, so Antonio did not mistake it for a coin Brin might have tried to keep. The ring was the *one* thing no one ever tried to take from him. Gypsies were too superstitious to risk taking something as important as a piece of jewelry left behind by the dead.

When he was satisfied that Brin had not kept any coins, Antonio dropped the pouch from his teeth and caught it in his right hand. With his other hand, he cuffed Brin again and gave him a kick to send him on his way.

"Mongrel," Antonio said. "Any other gypsy would have plucked double from those stupid geese of townspeople."

Antonio was lying. No gypsy had quicker or lighter hands than Brin, and many secretly envied him for his pickpocketing talent.

"You don't even earn what we feed you," Antonio continued. "You're lucky we don't leave you behind."

Brin walked away with as much dignity as he could. He didn't look back to see if Antonio was following to cuff him again, which happened more often than not.

"Get to the stream," Antonio snarled. "The women need help washing clothes. If I see you idling around camp, you'll get more of the back of my hand."

Brin turned obediently toward the stream. When he was safely from Antonio's sight, he allowed himself a smile. Beneath his tongue was a coin that Antonio had been unable to find. Brin popped it out of his mouth and tucked it into his pocket. Later he would add it to the many he had collected and hidden, one by one, over the last years.

Knowing he had fooled Antonio was the only consolation Brin could take, however. The blows still stung, and they reminded him how much worse it could get if he disobeyed Antonio.

He did not expect to be treated any better at the stream. The women would mock him, as they always did, for his fair skin and the dishonor of being fathered by someone who wasn't a gypsy.

And tonight he would get the few scraps left after all the gypsies had eaten their fill. He would be forced to eat alone in the shadows beyond the fire.

As he walked toward the stream, Brin remembered the stranger's question.

What do you seek?

What do I seek? Brin asked himself.

He sighed as the answer came to him immediately.

A home.

6

This night, as usual, Brin sat in the shadows beyond the campfires, waiting for the talk to die down and the gypsies to go to bed. He strained his ears to hear beyond their voices, counting the strikes of the bell that echoed from the town. When the bell struck eleven times, he began to feel restless. The stranger had said to meet him at midnight. He was tempted to bolt camp then, except there were occasions when the gypsy elders called him to answer Antonio's drunken accusations of laziness. This night more than any other Brin did not want his absence noticed. So he forced himself to wait.

The crackling wood finally became dull embers, and the last of the gypsies shuffled into their tents. Brin quietly slipped away.

He trotted slowly through the fields, letting his eyes adjust to the dim light from the moon and stars. Night held no fear for Brin. He almost thought of it as a friend, especially during the warmth of summer when he often roamed alone beneath the stars, taking pleasure from the soft air and the smell of fields and the buzzing of insects. At night, Brin thought of himself as a cat, padding lightly, alert to any sounds, and part of the rhythm of the breeze and the swaying grass.

Because he had forced himself to wait until all the gypsies had gone to bed, it was almost midnight when Brin reached the road along the river that would take him to the bridge. He would have liked to have arrived earlier at the bridge, to wait in the shadows to see if the hooded stranger came alone. Brin was not prepared to believe that anyone in the entire world would want to help him, and there were too many questions to be answered before he would trust a stranger.

He pushed himself to run as quickly as he could, but the last peals of the midnight bells had faded from the night air long before he finally reached the bridge. When Brin finally stepped out from the trees near the road, he saw no one. He feared he was too late.

He stepped farther into the road, leaving the safety of those comforting shadows.

Still, he saw no one.

But then he heard something.

A groan.

It came from the bridge!

The stones of the bridge formed an arch that rose from the road and then fell again to the other side of the river. The groan came from the side of the bridge hidden to Brin.

He hesitated in stepping onto the bridge. Although Brin did not fear the night, he did fear those who used the darkness for dangerous deeds. Brin knew that robbers and thieves preyed on those who walked these roads alone at night. Bridges were one of the best places for these bad men to ambush unwary travelers as they hurried to the town.

The groan grew louder and then faded into a sigh.

Was this a trap?

Brin thought of the man's words earlier in the day. *If it is harm I want to bring on you, all I need do is call and you will be taken away for stealing from the pockets of the townspeople. What could you, a poor gypsy boy, have of value to steal? Tonight, you shall see that it is an offer of help that I bring.*

If the stranger had wanted to harm Brin, he would have done so earlier.

Brin also thought of the reddish-blond beard that perhaps he had seen beneath the man's hood. A traveler from a faraway land? His father's land?

Brin would help.

As another groan rose from the other side of the bridge, Brin moved forward. Ahead, the fallen figure of a man came into view, half hidden against the wall of the bridge.

The stranger?

Brin hurried close and knelt beside the man.

"Is it you?" Brin asked. "The one who promised to help?"

The man attempted to roll toward Brin. His head fell back.

Brin lifted the man's head from the cold hard stones. He felt a slick warmth against his fingers.

Blood!

"Yes, it is I," the man whispered. "Betrayed. The enemy somehow knew I found you."

"The enemy?" Brin echoed. "Whom do you fight?"

"We fight them," the man groaned. "It is your fight too."

"My fight? But—"

"No," the man said with sudden strength. "You must run! Now! If they return…" He clutched at Brin's arm. "The girl will find you. Listen for one word. *Grail.*"

"Grail?"

"When you hear it, trust her."

Brin froze. Above the hoarse whispers of the fallen man, his ears had caught the shuffling of leather against stone. Footsteps.

"They have returned," the man said. "I told them you had come and gone, but they have returned. Now run!"

Brin hesitated.

"Run!" the man repeated with even more urgency. "It is not you they want but your ring."

The man pushed Brin away.

But it was too late. On one side of the bridge, two men appeared in outline against the night sky.

Brin turned to run the other way, but two men appeared from that side of the bridge as well.

He was trapped.

It was just as obvious to me as it is to you now that the four men—two on each side of the bridge—had unpleasant intentions for Brin.

Add it up. And don't go running for a calculator to do it. For centuries, humans your age had to do it the old-fashioned way—mentally—or by counting fingers. You can too. (Actually, I'm a big fan of calculators and computers. Watching over you when you do homework is very, *very* boring. The less time it takes you, the better for me. It's so much more exciting to be on guard duty when you're outside doing modern-day kid's stuff like skateboarding or rock climbing.)

Anyway, add it up. The mysterious hooded stranger is hurt. He's uttered a warning for Brin to run. Then there's this ambush on the bridge in the dark of night. Things are not looking good for Brin.

Maybe at this point you expect it's time for me to go into action—that it's my job to swoop in on mighty wings and then swoop away again from the bridge with Brin, setting him down somewhere safe.

No. No. No.

First, get this whole thing about angel wings out of your mind. Sure, there have been times when we appear that way to you. But come on. Real wings? With feathers and bones and tendons? Yuck. Ever watch birds closely enough to see the amount of work they have to spend on their wings? (Try the nature channel since you seem to be spending all that time in front of a television anyway.) There's grooming, oiling, and, worst of all, picking at those little lice things they eat.

Get this straight. Angels don't have real wings.

How did that myth get started, you ask?

Well, I'm more than happy to clear up the misconception. Think about this: Words are only symbols of reality.

Huh?

Look at it this way. Someone says to you it's raining cats and dogs. You certainly don't look up in the sky expecting to see the local pound dumping all their animals from an airplane. You know that the phrase "raining cats and dogs" really means it's raining really, really hard. Sometimes we use words in this creative way to describe what we're seeing.

Now pretend it's a situation where *nothing* in your experience has prepared you for what you're about to see. Like, if you were going to see an angel. Pretend you are someone in biblical times who sees this supernatural being, shimmering with light, for the first time. You don't fully comprehend all aspects of this angel, and, when you describe it later, you are forced to use mere words to explain something that is truly not describable with words. So you do the best you can with the words you have. You describe the shimmering light as wings because that's the best way you can figure out how to describe the indescribable.

So, one person describes the light surrounding us as looking like wings, the person hearing about it says to the next person this shimmering light is actually a set of wings. And they tell the next person that angels have wings! And when the artists get involved, forget it. Suddenly we're the stars of oil paintings in medieval churches everywhere, except we're looking like flocks of birds and we're flitting all over creation in search of seed.

That's harmless enough, I suppose. But look what you've done with the devil. He's been turned into a grinning red guy with horns and a pitchfork. Bad. Real bad. You've made a harmless cartoon character out of someone so evil it gives me the chills to think about it. (The good news is Satan is only temporary. Our Father totally defeats him at the end of time.)

All of this to say that one of the reasons I wasn't about to swoop down like a mighty eagle to rescue Brin is that I don't have wings—no matter what the paintings of angels look like. Got that? No wings.

The other reason is really more important, though.

Listen carefully: You are not on earth to be coddled and protected. If our Father sent us to take care of every problem you faced, how would you grow and learn?

For example, here's what happens when a baby learns to walk: A loving parent makes sure that the baby isn't at the edge of a cliff. Okay, that's an exaggeration, but you know what I mean. The parent only allows the baby to crawl in a room where there are no razor blades and no pieces of broken glass on the floor. And no pet cobras on the loose. Okay, those are exaggerations too.

What I'm trying to say is that a loving parent lets a baby crawl where it's safe. And when the baby takes his first little steps and falls, unless the baby is hurt and needs help, the parent allows the baby to struggle to his feet again. And fall again. That's how the baby learns to walk.

It will help you to think of your entire life as a series of baby steps. Once you learn how to do one thing, you move on to the next. Don't beat yourself up over mistakes when you're doing the best you can.

Unless you decide to do something wrong that you know has consequences. Then it's not a mistake. It's stupid.

In short, my duty as an angel is not to protect you from every bruise and bump. (Remember: *You* make the choices, not me.) But on occasion, when absolute disaster is about to hit—and if it's in our Father's will—an angel is sent to intervene. Like a parent who gently steers a baby away from the edge of the cliff. Or who makes sure the baby doesn't mistake dark brown things in the cat litter box for chocolate bars.

Our Father's will, however, might be to allow what appears to be a disaster to take place. And this apparent disaster won't make sense until, on the other side, you see how all the individual baby steps add up to your life's journey.

This is a really long way of saying that as I saw the two men approach Brin from each side of the bridge, I understood from our Father that this was not the time to protect him. This was a time to watch and wait to see if Brin could handle it himself.

If our Father's will was for me to step in and change the outcome, every aspect of my spiritual being would instantly sense it. And would sense how our Father wanted it accomplished.

Otherwise, Brin was on his own against the four of them...

7

What frightened Brin most was the silence of the men on each end of the bridge. They advanced slowly, as if with total certainty of purpose, total certainty that what they wanted was in their grasp.

In this silence and fear, all other sounds became magnified to Brin—the gurgle of the small river beneath the bridge, the wheezing breath of the fallen man, the pounding of Brin's heart. All reached him clearly as time seemed to stand still.

Step by step, quietly, slowly, the men grew closer.

Brin measured his distances. The bridge was too narrow to allow him room to dodge between the men. The drop to the river was too far, and the water too shallow.

At five steps away on each side, the men stopped.

Brin backed himself to the wall of the bridge, trying to keep them in his vision to his right and left.

All four men withdrew short swords from their capes.

"The ring, gypsy boy," said one of the men in a soft, deadly voice. "We mean to have it."

Brin could not imagine what importance the ring might have. Yet here were five men—four attacking, one fallen and motionless—who had suddenly appeared in Brin's life, and all of them sought the ring.

Yet Brin was not going to give it up. It was the only thing his parents had left him.

And, suddenly, in that moment on the bridge, Brin understood that the ring was the one thing, maybe the only thing, which could lead him to the secrets of his parents' lives. Whatever the secret of the ring, it was a secret they kept before dying. And if these men knew about the ring, they must also know about his mother and father.

"I do not have it with me," Brin said, trying to keep his voice from shaking. "It is back among the gypsies. Tell me why you seek it, and I will bring it to you tomorrow."

One man laughed. "Gypsies never tell the truth, even if they're only half gypsies fathered by a runaway knight. If we let you go, we'll never see you again."

Fathered by a runaway knight. The words echoed in Brin's mind. His father had been a knight! What else could Brin discover if he kept these men talking?

"My father did not run away," Brin said, thinking as quickly as he could. "He was sent on a mission of great importance."

"Bah," another said. "It was doomed from the beginning. Once he reached Rome, he would have been stopped."

Despite the danger, Brin felt a surge of triumph. He had outwitted these men into telling him more about his father. A knight who truly *had* been on a mission of great importance. With Rome as a destination. But what was the mission?

"If you had any idea how important that mission was," Brin began, hoping to learn more, "you would never say such a thing."

"Enough talk!" barked the first man. "The ring, gypsy. We know you carry it around your neck."

Brin's brain whirled. Could he fool these men again?

Slowly, he moved his left hand into his shirt pocket, hoping the darkness would conceal the motion of his fingers.

"Do not delay," the first man said. "Whether we take it from you dead or alive, we will take it."

"How is it you know I carry it?" Brin asked, easing his hand away again.

"We know. It is around your neck, on a strip of leather. Hand it over. Now."

With a sudden spin, Brin hopped onto the bridge wall. Looking over the edge and imagining the drop to the black water below dizzied him.

"Jump, then," the first man sneered, taking a step forward. "We'll strip the ring from your broken body."

Brin did not jump. Instead, he reached into his shirt and pulled the ring over his head. He dangled it in front of them.

"And if I throw this far into the river?" Brin asked. "You will never find it."

The man stopped. "Do that and you will only live long enough to watch us pull the entrails from your body."

"I wish to live," Brin said. He held the ring over the water. "Yet before I give it to you, tell me about my father."

"No!" The sudden shout from the fallen man on the bridge startled everyone. "At the cost of your life," he moaned, "keep the ring from them."

Brin ignored him.

"Tell me about my father," he continued. "A knight from where?"

"Scotland," came the answer. "A fiefdom in the wild moors of Scotland."

"What was his mission?"

"No more," the first man answered. "I tire of your games. Hand us the ring and we will let you live. Our fight is not with you."

But it is, Brin vowed silently, *for any fight of my father's is now a fight of mine.*

"You may have it," Brin said. With one hand on the ring and the other on the leather strap, he yanked and snapped it loose.

One man stepped closer and held out his hand.

"No..." the fallen man groaned. "Keep it from them."

"Here it is," Brin said to the men.

With a sleight of hand, Brin tossed the coin he had pulled from his pocket far over their heads. A few seconds later, a rolling clink reached all of their ears as it landed on the cobbles of the road.

Two of the men turned at the sound. In the dark, they could not see it was the coin and not the ring Brin had thrown.

It was all the distraction Brin needed.

He dove from the wall toward them and landed in a rolling somersault. Pain shredded his shoulder, but he kept moving. In a flash, he jumped to his feet and dodged past the men.

Something touched his forearm, burning a long slice through his skin.

A sword!

Brin sprinted.

Something plucked at his shirt, then landed with a clank ahead of him.

A thrown dagger!

Brin twisted and sidestepped, not losing speed, to the end of the bridge, dreading a blade in his back at any moment.

None came.

Brin burst from the bridge and ducked hard into the trees along the road. He plunged through the brush, climbed over a stone wall, and ran into the field. He felt like his feet were guided by angels, and he skimmed over the soft, grassy earth.

Finally, when his throat and lungs were raw, he allowed himself to look back.

No one chased him.

He had lost them all.

He slowed to a walk. As his breathing returned to normal, his mind went into action. These men knew too much about him. They'd known about the ring. They'd known where he kept it.

That information could only come from one place: the gypsy camp. Someone in the clan had betrayed him to a hated outsider.

Whatever miserable home Brin had had among the gypsies was no longer safe.

He was truly alone.

8

Brin slept poorly that night. He lay curled against a stack of hay in a field beyond the gypsy camp. The side of his forearm hurt badly from the thin wound caused by the sword. Whenever he rolled in his sleep, the movement cracked the new crust of dried blood and woke him. Each time he opened his eyes, the fright of his near death took him back to the bridge and all his questions.

The hurt stranger. Was he truly a friend? If he was, how could it be that they shared the same fight? And what was the fight?

The four men on the bridge. Why did they want the ring so badly? Who were they? How did they know of his father?

Behind all those questions, though, Brin found some satisfaction. He now knew more. His father, a knight! On a mission from Scotland! Comforted by this, Brin didn't feel so much like an orphan for the first time in his life.

Finally, when the pain woke him to the gray beginnings of a new day, Brin sat up and hugged his knees toward him. Distant roosters crowed triumph at the miracle of a rising sun. The gray sky brightened to blue, and yet Brin did not move.

He was tired, hungry, and thirsty, and his stiff muscles ached with the night cold that had not yet left his bones. But he would not move unless a peasant farmer happened to stray toward this particular stack of hay. He would wait until the gypsies packed their tents and cleared camp. That it would happen on this day, he was certain. The gypsy clan always departed the morning after Marcel's act upon the rope. The townspeople would have rightfully blamed the gypsies for the theft of their money. But with only suspicions instead of proof, it would take the entire day for the townsfolk to build their anger and courage to the point of going to the camp in the evening, usually armed with pitchforks and clubs. They would, of course, find nothing but ashes of fires, bones of chickens stolen from their farms, and grass matted where the tents had stood.

Brin, too, intended to arrive at a deserted camp. But he intended to arrive long before the townspeople, and he expected to find more than ashes and bones. He would reclaim what belonged to him.

9

"Do you need help?"

Although Brin felt his heart leap inside him like a startled rabbit, he forced himself to straighten slowly to the soft, pleasant voice behind him.

A girl's voice.

He put a calm look on his face before turning. After all, if she had meant immediate harm, she would have acted instead of spoken. Whatever answer Brin gave her, he preferred to do so without showing weakness of fear.

Brin finally faced her. Behind him was a fire pit, long cold since the departure of the gypsies. In his hand, he held the broken stick he had been using to dig into the ashes.

"There is blood on your clothing," she said, "and straw in your hair. You stir a fire, yet I see no flames. I find all of this curious."

His questioner looked about his age. She wore the fine clothes of royalty and sat astride a white horse. Her hair was long and reddish blonde and tied neatly behind her shoulders.

Brin almost bowed to her, such was her manner.

"I am sorry to be an intruder on your field," Brin said, assuming she was the daughter of the landowner. "I shall leave immediately."

"Before or after you find what you sought in the dead fire?"

Brin kept his face frozen. He did not want his expression to betray how badly he needed what was hidden in the earth below the ashes.

"Do not answer," she said with the trace of a smile at his discomfort. "Instead, let me ask again. Do you need help?"

"I need nothing from any person," he said. "I need only to be alone."

"I find that an interesting lie," she frowned. "How do you intend to flee the four men who approach on horseback?"

She pointed behind him. He followed her arm with his eyes. He saw only the stone fence at the distant edge of the field and the rising hills beyond.

"There are no horsemen," he said.

"Were there not four men last night?"

How did she know?

"And if I could find you so easily," she said, "they will too. Where else would you go but to this camp? They will be on horses and coming from the town."

"Who are you?" Brin asked, suddenly afraid.

"Your guardian angel."

Brin shrank from her.

She laughed. "It is only a figure of speech. I am sorry. I had forgotten how strongly the gypsies cling to old stories and superstitions."

"You are here to guard me?" he asked.

"In a manner of speaking, yes." She smiled. "Those men on horseback seek the ring."

The ring. Brin immediately became guarded. If she knew about the ring…

He looked beyond her to the trees along the stream at the other side of the field and the faraway woods past the stream.

"Were I you," she said, reading his mind, "I would not flee. Yes, before they arrive, escape is likely. Yet escape will not solve your problem. No matter where you travel, their spies will find you. They will seek you day and night. They will not rest until they have the ring."

"I cannot give them what I do not have," Brin said boldly. "Last night, I tossed it into the darkness."

"You tossed a coin," she countered. "You are quick-minded. I admire you for it."

How did she know this? And so quickly?

"I cannot give them what I do not have," Brin repeated. First a hooded stranger. Now this girl on horseback. Both of them knowing about the ring. Mystery overwhelmed him. His best path seemed to be in keeping his own secrets.

"They believe you still have it as well," she said. "They will torture you until you give it up to them. Or until they are satisfied you do not have it."

"What do you know of the ring?" Brin asked. "Why do you offer to help me?"

"The story is far too long to tell now," she said. "If you want to hear it, you must travel with me."

"Where?"

"That too is part of the story I will tell as we travel."

"No," Brin said. His muscles ached. He was cold, hungry, and thirsty. He was tired of these games with words. He did not trust her. Perhaps she was only after the ring like the others. "I will find my own way."

"To where?" she asked. "Back to the gypsies? It appears you have left them."

"Why should you care?" Brin said. "My life is my own."

"Your path matters much to me," she said softly. "And your life is not your own. Or have you no faith in our heavenly Father?"

"Must you speak in riddles?"

"I will stop," she said as she pointed. "They approach."

Indeed, there were four men. They were beyond the far edge of the field, coming toward Brin on black horses.

"Choose between me and them," she said. "You might have your doubts about me, but they are merely doubts. Of them, on the other hand, you can be certain they mean you harm."

There was no choice for Brin.

"How can you help me?" he asked.

"Give them what they seek," she said. "Once they have it, they will no longer pursue you."

"I have already told you that—"

Brin stopped, cut short by the motions of her hand as she tossed him a round piece of metal. He snapped it from the air and glanced at it.

The ring.

"It is a close copy, is it not?" she asked.

Brin studied it. It was the same size and had similar markings, but it was not identical.

"A close copy," he agreed.

"My advice to you," she said, "is to give it up reluctantly. That will convince them that it is the ring they seek."

"After that?"

"Once they leave, go to the stream. You will see a tall tree, once struck with lightning and now white from years of weather. Wait for me there."

"What if they kill me?" Brin asked. His sore arm was a reminder of how close they had come to succeeding the night before.

"Look," she said. "They wear masks."

Brin looked. Far away as they were, he could see their faces were covered with dark cloth.

"The masks show they wish to remain unknown to you. Would they go to such effort if they intended to kill you? No. They seek only the ring. To them, you are merely a pawn."

"And to you?" he asked.

The four horsemen had reached the stone fence, perhaps a half mile distant.

"That is a fair question. Yes, to us, you are also a pawn. It will be a great service to us if you mislead them with this false ring. Yet you are more than a pawn. You will have the opportunity to test yourself and join us if your heart is right."

"Us?" he asked.

The drumming of horse hooves reached him faintly. His attention, though, remained on her.

"Those who sent your father into this far land."

Again. His father!

"Who?" Brin demanded. "Who are you?"

She turned the horse with a flick of the reins. She looked back at him and uttered five simple words before riding away from him and the approaching horsemen.

"Keepers of the Holy Grail."

There. *Finally*, you think. You now know the extremely important reason that our Father sent me into Brin's life.

The Holy Grail! The cup that Jesus used in His Last Supper! Something that people have searched for over the last 20 centuries!

Boring. Boring. Boring. Your human ideas of what's important are often ridiculous.

I wish you could fully understand what truly matters to our Father. Your precious souls, not some cup. End of story.

But I'll explain anyhow.

In light of all the centuries of human history, the life and death of an old beggar in the slums of some big city might seem so unimportant that it would be beyond notice. Yet my greatest glory and honor to our Father has come on the occasions when He sent me to protect such beggars from untimely deaths. Even with people as poor and dirty and unnoticed as beggars, our Father wanted to give them one more chance to live long enough to choose faith in our Father and join us in the Eternal Home. And upon their arrival after they did die, each of those beggars—unknown to you but infinitely treasured by our Father—received such a joyous welcome that it was as if there had been no other soul ever saved in such a way.

Still, you say, surely this time my mission had something to do with the Holy Grail.

Maybe. But I wasn't going to get too excited about the possibility.

Boys and girls, the Holy Grail is just a cup! After what I've just explained about human souls, do you still think our Father places any significance in lifeless lumps of metal?

Let me repeat: Our Father loves your souls. He wants to give you every chance possible to reach for Him. That's all it takes—reach for Him. (To more fully understand this concept, read the Gospels and how our Father saved your souls by letting His Son accept the punishment you deserve for turning away from Him.)

Still stuck on the Holy Grail as the important part of my mission?

There are lots of reasons our Father sends us among you. I've been on countless missions over the centuries, and I have listened to other angels describe their missions to me.

Sometimes, yes, it's immediately apparent why our Father wants us involved. Let me just say that World War II, as you've called it, kept many, many, *many* of us busy. For a while, Satan thought he had a good thing going with Hitler and the concentration camps. I shudder to think what would have happened had Hitler managed to put together a world empire. But enough of you made the right choices, and evil was defeated.

Other times a mission might seem totally unneeded.

Take a kid about 900 years ago. He grew up in an area of Europe that would later become Germany. He had ten brothers and sisters, and they were such a big brood that the mother, a widow, could hardly keep track of them. This kid had a thing about climbing trees. Big trees, little trees, old trees. Didn't matter to him. He just wanted to climb. And he always did it when his mother was busy with another brother or sister. Boy, did he keep me busy for a stretch of five years. Then one day, he got over the tree-climbing thing. It wasn't because he'd fallen; no, I made sure he was safe each time. He just decided to quit. And only then was I called back to the glory of our Father's presence.

Much as I wanted to ask our Father why I'd been put to all that work for a little tree-climber, I just waited. And waited. (It's not really "waiting," though, because time is much different on our side than yours.) I saw first that the kid gave his soul to our Father about ten years after my mission was over. There was another big celebration when he stepped through death's curtain and showed up among us. And I've been very mature ever since—I haven't once burst his bubble and explained it was me, and not his great athletic skill, that kept him safe during his tree-climbing years.

Still, I wondered if there had been more to my mission than that. Then 376 years later, his great-great-great-great-great-great-great-great-great-great-grandson was born. November of AD 1483. The grandson didn't seem like much to anyone around him. But I'd been sent to watch over him, and the world would need him soon enough. (Trust me, our Father has a great sense of humor. He knew all along I'd been wondering about that little tree-climber who was such a rascal, and I was about to get the answer.) See, all those centuries later, in November of 1483, after the long line of families who were all offspring of that tree-climber, comes this boy named Martin. You may have heard of him. Last name was Luther. If that tree-climber nearly 400 years earlier had fallen and broken his neck, we wouldn't have had one of the most important people in church history. He stood up for God and truth and turned people back to our Father.

Get the idea?

Every mission is important.

Just not always the way you might expect.

Still, hearing the girl talk about the Holy Grail did make me curious. Century after century, enough of you humans have made fools of yourselves searching for it that I knew, as you often say, the plot was about to thicken.

10

The mysterious girl had been right.

The horsemen let Brin live. They took the fake ring and departed without striking a blow or uttering a threat.

As the morning sun grew hot, Brin worked at his task at the fire. He kept digging until he found his treasure. Beneath the ashes, protected by a thick layer of packed dirt, was his leather pouch of coins.

Brin had secretly saved the money over the years. Marcel's father Antonio always searched Brin's clothing after he pick-pocketed the townspeople, but Brin usually hid one coin beneath his tongue. As his collection grew, he had to find clever hiding spots for his coins. Since he was in charge of preparing the fire pit, he often chose to hide the coins deep in the soil beneath the fire, knowing no gypsy would stumble upon his treasure there.

With the coin pouch safely in his hand, Brin felt much better. To be sure, he had no home, and the feeling of sadness surprised him. The gypsies taunted him, sometimes beat him, and they always treated him as worse than a slave. Why would he be sad that he was no longer with them?

Because it's the only life I've known, he admitted to himself. Part of him wanted to set off in pursuit of the clan. Better to be lonely among them, he figured, than alone in unknown dangers.

What held Brin back, however, was the knowledge that someone among the gypsies had betrayed him to the hooded stranger. It didn't matter if the stranger's intentions were good; Brin had been betrayed by someone in the clan. He could never go back.

Should he take his coins and wander? Perhaps a farmer might give Brin work. Or he could learn a trade. If he worked very hard, perhaps one day he could have a home to call his own. And if fortune really blessed him, he might even marry and have a family.

The thought made him smile. A home and family of his own was one of his favorite daydreams.

But he was equally drawn to the mysterious girl. Not her looks, he scolded himself, but the promise of what she knew about his father.

Should he risk traveling with her?

Although Brin thought about the question for a while, he knew deep down that there was only one answer.

Yes. He would travel with her. He had too many questions. If he turned his back on them now, he would regret it his entire life, regardless of what fortune brought him.

Questions.

How could she have known that Brin had tossed a coin and not the ring onto the cobblestone at the bridge? Only the hooded stranger and the four men would have known that. But if she had learned this from the four men, why had she helped Brin trick them again? No, the hooded stranger had to have told her. They must be friends if not partners.

The hooded stranger knew of Brin's father. As did the girl. That alone drew Brin to them.

And the secret behind the ring. Why were men willing to risk their lives for it? How could it matter so much that men were willing to kill?

And who were these Keepers of the Holy Grail? Why had they sent Brin's father into this land?

Brin was determined to learn the answers.

Even at the risk of his life.

He would go carefully, however, trusting no one.

Brin walked to the stream. He washed himself, glad for the cool water.

He searched for the tall, white tree and found it downstream, only a hundred paces away. Brin settled himself into the shade of the tree, and despite his best intentions, he fell asleep.

He dreamed a dark dream. He was falling, falling, falling into a deep, black hole. When he hit bottom, his arms and legs could not move, and flies tormented him by crawling on his face, flies he could not wave away. In his dream, his tongue grew thick with thirst until a gentle singing voice pulled him out of the deep black hole.

Brin woke, blinking, to a damp cloth smoothed over his cheeks and forehead.

It took him a moment to realize the gentle song was not part of the dream but belonged to a girl who cradled his head and soothed his face.

It was the mysterious girl.

11

She smiled.

"You're awake," she said. "I feared you might never return."

Brin pushed himself to a sitting position. He croaked with surprise to see the long shadows of evening upon him.

"The sun! Nearly gone! Surely I haven't slept all day!"

"I doubt it was sleep," she said. "More likely, you have been drugged."

Brin tried standing. His legs failed him and he sat again.

"My head hurts. My tongue is a block of wood."

"Drugged then," she said. "I have been with you a good part of the afternoon, shading your face from the sun."

"Drugged?" He thought of the sensation of arms and legs like blocks of wood, of flies crawling across his face. "But why?"

"I don't know," she said, "but I fear the worst."

"The worst?"

"Your ring," she said. "Someone searched you for it."

"How could that be?" Every answer she gave him only led to more questions. "Those horsemen believe they have it."

"Did you lose the ring?" she asked, ignoring his question. "Was it taken from you while you slept?"

Brin patted himself, searching. He found the pouch of coins and relaxed a little. If indeed he had been searched for the ring, the searcher was not a common thief.

"I told you earlier that I did not have the ring," he scowled. "How could I have lost it then?"

"As you say," she said.

"Without the ring, am I of less value to you?"

"Every living soul has value to our Father in heaven," she said.

Again, she spoke of heaven. The gypsies had taught Brin that it was fortune who smiled or frowned at whim, not a God in heaven.

"Aside from my value to this Father of yours," Brin said, "without the ring, am I still of use to you?"

She dropped the damp cloth and stood, helping Brin to his feet. He saw her white horse grazing nearby, reins tied to a branch.

"Come to the stream," she said. "Drink."

The sun's light had become golden. It was the quiet part of evening when the wind died and the green of the trees and fields grew soft and shadowed.

Somehow, being with this girl made Brin more aware of all the beauty around him.

Stop thinking like that! he commanded himself inwardly. There was *nothing* he would trust about this girl. It could have been her who drugged him and searched him. After all, she was the one who had directed him to that oak; she knew where to find him. For that matter, he didn't even know her name.

"What should I call you?" he said.

"Rachel," she said.

"You know I'm Brin?"

She nodded.

Brin crouched at the stream, filled his hands with water, and gulped again and again. After taking his fill, he asked again. "Rachel, without the ring, am I still of use to you and the Keepers of the Grail?"

He already knew the answer. Of course he was of use to her. Why else would she have stayed with him the afternoon? Especially if it had been her who had searched him for the ring and discovered it gone. He was simply asking to judge her reply.

She answered his question with a question. "If I supplied you with a good reason, would you be able to trace the ring's markings on paper with charcoal?"

Brin thought of the days he had stared at the ring, and the nights he had held it in the darkness, running his fingers over the upraised symbols. It was all that held him to his dead parents. The markings were seared into his mind.

"I am able," he said.

"And will you travel with me to Rome?"

Rome. The greatest city in all mankind. Despite his hurting head and great thirst, excitement surged through Brin. *The city that his father had been sent to on a mission.*

"Yes," he answered. "If you tell me about my father as we travel."

"Then," she told him, "you have great value. Greater than you can imagine."

12

Rachel let Brin sit behind her on the white horse. He thrilled at the prospect—he had never been on a horse before. Only the wealthy were afforded such luxurious travel.

Yet a few miles later, Brin decided the wealthy could keep horses for themselves. He sat squarely upon the spine of the beast, and it was not comfortable at all.

"Do we ride to Rome tonight?" he asked. "If so, perhaps I will walk beside this horse."

"Hardly," she laughed. "There is a monastery just over the next hill. We are guests there."

"We?"

"My brother and I," Rachel answered. "Edwin. You met him yesterday. First in town. Then at the bridge."

Brin felt secret relief. He had not dared ask about the hooded stranger, fearing she might tell him the man was her husband or her betrothed.

"He is not hurt badly, then." Brin said it not as a question, but as an observation.

"He suffered a cracked head and must rest for a week or two. But the monks who nurse him assure me his injury does not threaten his life." She paused.

"How did you know he wasn't hurt badly?"

"You showed no signs of worry or grief."

"Gypsy," she said, "it bodes well that you watch things closely and use logic as a tool. I shall welcome your help."

Brin cautioned himself against enjoying the warmth of her praise.

"Again," he said rather roughly, "let me ask you to tell me about my father."

Rachel laughed once more. "And again, let me tell you that one more night matters little. At the monastery, you shall be fed well. You will be invited to bathe, and after a complete night's rest, you and I will begin our journey."

"Just the two of us?"

"Just the two of us," she answered.

"No soldiers to guard us?"

"You are a gypsy, accustomed to living by your wits. What do you fear?"

Brin nearly gave the answer closest to the tip of his tongue. What he feared was what he did not know about her.

"It is not usual for a young woman to travel unattended," he replied instead. "Bandits along the road will see us as easy prey."

"They will not see a young woman," she said.

"I don't understand."

"Because we must leave Edwin behind to rest and heal," Rachel said, "you and I will travel as beggars. Do you fancy the guise of an old man or an old woman?"

"What!"

She laughed again. It was a sound that, against his will, Brin was growing to like. "An old man, then," she said. "We shall keep one of your arms beneath your shirt. It will appear as though you are maimed. Better to be seen as totally helpless." She shifted on the horse. "As for me, I shall pretend to be your wife, still faithful after years of poverty. Does that suit you?"

"Answers suit me," he growled. "And thus far you have strung me along as a donkey follows the carrot on the end of a stick."

More light laughter from Rachel. "You said it, gypsy, not I!"

Yes, indeed, Brin was right. Rachel was stringing him along like a donkey follows the carrot on the end of the stick.

It's probably just as obvious to you as it was to me that the carrot he was chasing was a lot more than the answers he thought she could give him about his father. He just wanted to fool himself into believing there was nothing more going on. That he wasn't really about to act like a donkey.

But there *was* something more going on, wasn't there? And like most guys, he was going to have a hard time not making a donkey of himself as he tried to figure it out.

Yes, boys and girls. We're talking *l-o-v-e*. In capital letters.

L-O-V-E.

My, oh, my. Have I seen plenty of that over the centuries.

Angels are complete in the glory of the presence of our Father. We weren't built like you. You know, where one and one equals one. Don't pretend you don't understand. I don't mean the kissy-smoochy stuff. I mean the joining of the hearts of one man and one woman in a relationship blessed by our Father, suddenly becoming so complete as partners they are like one person.

We aren't built like you, but we angels talk. We compare notes. This boy-girl stuff is fascinating.

On one hand, it looks so wonderful that if we weren't complete in the glory of the presence of our Father, we'd understand what it means to yearn for something.

On the other hand, we've seen you mess up our Father's incredible gift so many times that we're very glad *not* to get mixed up in any of it.

LOVE. Joy and heartache. Elation and desolation. Hope and despair.

I think boy-girl love is one of the most complicated things I've seen in the universe. (Even more complicated than, say, the dance of electrons and protons around the nucleus of the uranium atom, and believe me, that's complicated. Only our Father could have created the basic forces of the universe to work in such harmony—electromagnetism, the strong and weak nuclear forces, and gravity. I'm losing you here with quantum physics, aren't I? Sorry. But on the other side, you'll sense how our Father put it all together, and you'll spend all of eternity marveling at it like we do.)

My advice about LOVE?

Love is a fire. Under control—in the stove in a kitchen, for example—a fire's warmth is wonderful. Out of control or abused, a small fire will become a disaster that burns your house down.

Aach. Forget I just told you that. It's true, of course, but chances are you're going to learn about it the hard way no matter what anyone tells you. Heartbreak is not easy. But heartbreak you can get over, even though at the time it seems impossible. It's when you mess up physically before you're in a marriage and before you're ready to have your own children that love, or what you think is love, can really hurt you. And the people around you.

So if you're going to forget my advice, just like you'll probably want to ignore the advice of anyone older than you, at least forget one other thing—most of what you see in movies. Love is not what a man and woman do with each other. It's what they do *for* each other.

That's the way our Father intended His great gift for you.

As for Brin, he was clearly smitten already, even if he wasn't going to admit it to himself.

I almost envied him.

And certainly felt sorry for him...

13

An old woman woke Brin on his sleeping mat in a bare room in the monastery. Brin fell back in surprise as the crone's face loomed over him. Her nose was long and twisted, her skin gray and scarred. There was a filthy cape pulled over her head.

What repelled him most, however, was her smell.

Without thinking, Brin put his hand over his nose.

"I'm not the woman of your dreams?" the crone whispered.

He shook his head, blushing as if the old woman had read his mind. The woman of his dreams rode a white horse, had long reddish-blonde hair, and looked nothing like this smelly old—

"Rachel!" Brin said, suddenly remembering their conversation the night before. "Is that you?"

The old woman cackled briefly, then dropped her voice to normal tones.

"None other," Rachel said.

"This is astounding," Brin said.

"Well-placed wax and plant dyes," she said. "We Keepers of the Grail have a habit of altering our appearance. Lord Thomas told me many such stories. His own father was in disguise. Indeed that is how he first met his wife, Katherine." Rachel lost herself in daydream thoughts for a moment, as if she was remembering the tales as they were told to her. She shook herself to bring herself back to the present. "But those tales…"

Brin grinned, still holding his nose at her stench. "I know now that you are dangling a carrot. But I refuse to ask more questions until we are on the road to Rome."

"You learn quickly," she said. She dropped some clothes on the floor. "Wear these. You will get accustomed to the smell."

"Must the garments be so repulsive?"

"It will keep strangers from prying too closely," she said. "Rome is but a week away. We will not suffer long."

Brin groaned.

Rachel cackled again. "Hurry, my husband. Already the sun has risen. While you dress, I will visit Edwin and wish him well on his recovery. He has promised to follow and meet us in Rome as soon as he is able."

Brin's brow wrinkled. "Rome is a city of untold thousands and thousands and thousands. How will he find us there?"

"Do not fear," she said. "All you need to do is trust me."

———

During their first hour of travel, Rachel repeatedly corrected Brin for his habit of walking like a young man. As passersby approached, she would urge to him to stoop his back, lean on his crooked walking stick and to put the impression of pain into his steps.

Thus, to any observers, they appeared as poor, aged peasants. Once the road cleared of other travelers, however, both straightened and walked with rapid, firm steps.

It was a pleasant morning, with a light haze in the sky. Enough of a breeze passed over them to keep them cool, and, more importantly, to take away the stench of their filthy clothing.

"We have the ancient Romans to thank for our ease of travel," Rachel told Brin.

"Why is that?" Brin asked, reminding himself not to enjoy her company until the time might come that he could trust her.

"Perhaps you have heard the expression 'all roads lead to Rome'?"

He nodded, although he had not. Life among the gypsies did not provide much in the way of learning.

"Well," Rachel said, "all roads *do* lead to Rome. It was a great empire, controlling lands thousands of miles away. To rule, however, the Romans needed to be able to move armies in quickly at the first sign of revolt. They built cobblestone roads that stretched to all points of the empire. An army of thousands could arrive within two or three months. Such quick action not only stopped revolts but discouraged the provincial rulers from even starting trouble."

There was a long stretch of empty road ahead of them, stretching to the top of a slowly rising hill.

Rachel let her thoughts wander. "The Romans were intelligent in their politics. You see, they did not believe in ruling by force, but by threat of force, which takes much less effort. And unlike other empires, they did not strive for total domination of a conquered country. Instead, each country was allowed its own rulers, own customs, and own religions, as long as it continued to pay taxes and tribute to Rome."

Much as Brin wanted to push her to talk about the Keepers of the Grail, he found himself soaking in the knowledge like a thirsty plant. He considered what she had just told him.

"I think I understand," Brin said after a few minutes. "If you choose force as the way to control, then you must send in an army to occupy the lands. If it takes one army to control one country, and you have only ten armies, then you can subdue only ten countries. But if you rule the way the Romans did— without sending in your armies to occupy the land—then you can add far more than ten countries to your empire. And your ten armies are free to rove where needed." He grinned in triumph. "On roads that let them move quickly."

Rachel applauded. "You are an excellent student. I can see our time to Rome will pass quickly."

They passed a few more minutes in silence. No travelers appeared over the crest of the hill. They continued to walk quickly.

"Think on this," Rachel said. "Our Father in heaven placed His Son on earth during the one time in all of history that the world itself was best poised to allow men to spread His gospel. Had Jesus Christ been born even 50 years before, it would have been too early, for the Romans had yet to subdue Judea. Yet by the time He had been crucified, His followers could take His message out of Judea on Roman roads into the largest empire the world had ever known. And best of all, this was the first great empire that gave its people the freedom to choose their own religions. This was the one time, then, that the gospel could have a chance to take root. And of all those local religions, the one true faith endured and grew through the centuries that followed. How ironic, that this great empire, which crucified the Son of God, would soon worship Him."

She stopped. Brin's face showed puzzlement even beneath the heavy disguise of old age.

"Yes?" she asked.

"Heavenly Father? Son? Son of God?"

Rachel grew quiet for a few moments before speaking again. "Please forgive me," she said. "I forget you grew up among gypsies. Who there would have told you about the Christ?"

She shook her head, continuing to admonish herself. "We who have the faith sometimes assume everyone knows the story, and that those who don't believe persist in unbelief out of stubbornness. Instead, I suppose, we need to take the other's view and wonder what needs to be spoken. The message must be heard and understood before it can be believed."

"Message?" Brin laughed. "You have really lost me now."

"I suppose I have," she said. "But Rome is a week away, and I will tell you all about—"

"The Keepers of the Grail," Brin interrupted. "And how it is you have such knowledge of times past. I have been a dutiful donkey thus far, letting you dangle the carrot in front of my nose to bring me along this road. I will go no farther unless you begin to tell me as promised."

"Yes, I will tell you," she said. "All of it. And soon. But first we need to find our way past those men ahead. I fear their intentions are not the most kindly."

Brin turned his attention from her to the road. He saw the outline of five men who had crested the hill, a quarter mile ahead.

As they grew closer, it was obvious by their clubs and swords that they were highway bandits, confident that the isolation of this stretch of road made any travelers easy prey.

14

"What do we do?" Brin asked. His first impulse was to flee. He was not big, but he was fast. Yet if he outran Rachel, she would be alone against these bandits.

As a gypsy, Brin knew well the dangers of open countryside. These men could beat, rob, and kill Rachel. They could toss her body into a grove of trees. It might be days or weeks until a passerby happened to notice. And what of it? Who would waste effort searching for the bandits? No one. There was no threat of punishment, no threat of avenging soldiers to stop these men. Without a way for the countryside to be policed, solitary travelers always faced this risk.

If he ran, she faced death. If he stayed, they both faced death. What should he do?

The men walked purposefully toward them. Brin looked back over his shoulder. The road stretched down the long hill. Empty of all other travelers.

"What do we do?" Rachel asked. "We continue to walk toward them."

"But—"

"Fear not," she said. "Keepers of the Grail have many weapons."

"You have no sword," he said. "And even if you did, there are five against us."

The men were now a couple hundred yards away.

"Sword? Too crude." She placed a hand on his arm. "There is a marvelous substance called black powder, which most of Europe has yet to discover. Charcoal, sulphur, and saltpeter. When sparked, it explodes with fearsome force, sending a flash of white fire that can almost kill a man. I have some of that in my bag beneath this cloak."

"Use it!"

"Or perhaps a sleeping potion," she said, ignoring him. "Much more ladylike, don't you think? I have this hollow reed I can hide in my hand. With a puff of air from my mouth, a small dart flies forth, tipped with the potion. Just a scratch from this dart and and a man falls as if struck dead. It appears to be magic and will terrify those still standing. I have used this before."

"The potion, then!" To Brin, the five men seemed as menacing as an entire army. "Use the potion!"

She reached into her cloak. "I think not."

"Then the black exploding powder. They will be upon us soon."

"No," she said. "I prefer the most powerful weapon of all. Wits."

"Excellent," Brin said, slumping his shoulders in resignation. "We shall flay them with our wits. Most probably they will flee for their lives."

"Actually," Rachel answered, "despite your mocking tone, I believe they will."

Rachel pulled a small pouch out of the bag beneath her cloak.

"Turn with me, away from them," she instructed Brin. As he did, she opened the top of the pouch and poured red powder into her hand.

"Bring your face to my hand," she told Brin.

"What?"

"Step closer."

As he did, she brought her open hand up to his nose, so that the tips of her fingers almost touched his face.

"Do you see anything in this powder?" she asked.

Brin almost crossed his eyes to focus, so close was it to him. The powder was fine, like dust.

"I cannot see anything but —"

With a sudden and unexpected breath, she blew the powder into his eyes.

The blinding pain staggered him. He reached up to rub his stinging eyes. She grabbed his wrists and blocked his efforts.

"Quiet," she commanded. "Let the powder do its work."

"Have you lost your mind?" he snarled, yanking his wrists away. "I am not the one about to attack! Why did you—"

A sneeze took him, a sneeze of such proportion he almost lost his balance. Then another sneeze. Yet one more.

His eyes began to water so badly that tears streamed down his face. A few seconds later, his nose ran too.

More sneezing took him. He could hardly find breath. The next minutes passed as hours. Rachel would not let him wipe away the tears and mucus which flowed from his eyes and nose.

Finally, between sneezes, he saw that the bandits had arrived and stood less than ten paces away. But he could not see them clearly. The flood of tears blurred what he could see of them.

"Help us," croaked Rachel. "Good men, please help us!"

Help, wondered Brin. When men joined together like this, it was not to help those they found alone.

Brin sneezed, widely spraying the contents of his nose.

"We only need a little food," Rachel pleaded in a screeching voice. "Our only way of life is to beg, and the last town sent us away. How can we beg unless we are among people?"

The bandits did not move closer.

"You kind souls are the only ones not to show fear of my husband," Rachel said in her wavering voice. "He does not have the plague. I promise. They were wrong to send us away."

"Plague?" This uncertain question came from one of the bandits. Brin could not decide which, for again a sneezing fit took him.

"Do not be deceived by the red of his face," Rachel said, desperation in her voice. "It is not the fever of Black Death. He is in great health."

"Black Death?" another echoed.

Brin coughed and sneezed.

"Can you spare us anything?" she asked. She wobbled on her cane toward them. "Please, just give me…"

Through the blur of his tears, Brin saw them edge away.

"Don't leave," she cried. "Come closer, not farther. Some bread, some coin—that is all I ask."

As one body, all five men turned. They fell over themselves in their scramble to run. Their footsteps clattered on the cobblestone, rapidly growing farther away.

"Did I not tell you?" Rachel asked in merry tones. "They flee for their lives. Already they are almost out of sight."

Moments later, Brin felt hands on his face as Rachel gently placed a cloth on his nose and eyes.

"Take this," she said. "Wipe away those tears. Soon the effects of the powder will pass."

Brin dropped the cloth. He spun and began walking down the hill.

"Keep it," he said in forceful tones. "Keep your black powder and your potions. Keep your tricks and disguises."

"Brin!" She hurried after him.

"What you did was not right," he said, anger obvious in every stride.

"I did not lie," she protested, hard-pressed to stay with him. "I told them you were in good health. I am not to blame that they assumed you carried the plague."

"What was not right was how you treated me," he said. "From the moment I met your brother until now, you both have treated me like a child, teasing me with the promise of secrets, herding me like you would a sheep. Now this! Using me with your little trick of powder. Had you asked, I would have agreed. Our lives were in danger. But to blow it in my eyes without warning is…is…is…"

Brin could not remember the last time that anger had taken him to the point of rage. The gypsies had beaten him, taunted him, humiliated him, yet he always bore it with stoic patience. With them, however, he always understood they were clearly against him. Rachel, on the other hand, had pretended something different and then deceived him.

She placed her hand on his arm.

He shook it off. "I will never hit a girl," he said. "That is the only reason I am not striking you now."

"Please," she said softly. "We must not fight. As two who share the Grail's birthright, we must join together in the battle against evil."

Brin stopped. Grail *birthright?*

"Tell me everything," he said. "Now. Upon this hillside. I move no farther unless I hear it all."

15

They moved to sit in the shade of a tree. Brin's face itched from the waxy disguise, but he remained still. He so wished to know what she might say. It seemed to his ears that each of his heartbeats were separate peals of thunder.

"Let me begin," she said, "by telling you we have more in common than our birthright. When I hear the children sing the dance of death, I fight to hold back tears. My mother was taken by the Black Death, just like yours. This was a few years ago when the plague swept through England again."

Both of them gave respectful silence to her words. It was the single greatest fear in any person's mind. The bandits had fled from Brin and his red face and hard sneezes for good reason.

Black Death.

It was a plague which struck so quickly that a person might wake sneezing in the morning and be dead by nightfall.

Black Death.

It spread like fire touched to straw. All it took was one child in a family to begin the dreaded coughing, sneezing, and high fever and half, sometimes more, in that family would be dead within a week.

Black Death.

Towns of 500 would be reduced to 300 mourners, with the bodies of the 200 dead stacked in the streets to be burned as soon as the survivors found strength.

Black Death.

It took its name from those who died, their faces purple and dark in agony.

Black Death.

Half the population of Europe dead from two separate epidemics. Brin's parents taken in the first one in 1348. Rachel's mother taken in the next, 1361. Dead in the millions upon millions. A disease that struck commoner and royalty alike.

Black Death.

Red, rosy faces pocked with rings of pus. Pockets and sleeves stuffed with flowers, for it was futilely hoped that the scent would ward off the disease. The ashes of bodies burned. And the near certainty of falling down dead once the disease struck. Children now danced and sang a mockery of the death's darkness, the dance of death that always brought Rachel near tears as she remembered her dying mother. "Ring around the rosy," the children would say, "pockets full of posy, ashes, ashes, we all fall down."

The breeze of the hillside passed over them. In the sunshine, which had burned through the earlier haze, the horror of sweeping death seemed unreal. Yet not even the pleasantness of a morning alone in the countryside could banish the fear of that horror.

It took several minutes before Brin spoke.

"By your own words and by your accent," he said, "it is plain you come from a faraway land. You know, however, my mother fell to the plague. You know about my ring. You even knew that I plucked coins from the pockets of townspeople. How can all of this be? Will you at least tell me that?"

"Yes," Rachel said, "This answer is in a letter."

Brin waited. A butterfly dipped and swooped between them. Rachel finally took her eyes from it and answered his unspoken question.

"It was a letter from your father. It took years to reach us, passed and sold from traveler to traveler."

"Sold?"

"The bearer of this letter was promised half a year's wages for safe delivery to our small monastery in Scotland. Whoever first had the letter decided not to risk the danger of passing through many lands but instead sold it for a little gold to another who might take it closer. That person in turn sold it again. And so on. Each time the letter moved closer to our land. Once, though, its owner was killed by road bandits. And the bandit who took the dead man's possessions could not read and had no idea of the value of the letter. He discarded it. A little boy found it and brought it to his priest, the only man in the village who could read. The priest set it aside and forgot it. Not until the priest died several years later did anyone see it again, finding it among his books. And so the letter's journey resumed, until finally, many years after your father's death, his words reached us."

"And?" Brin said.

She didn't reply immediately.

Brin's patience could not be stretched further. "Why had he been sent into this land?" he demanded. "What of my mother? How did they meet? How did they fall in love? How did he die? What sent her back to the gypsies without him?"

Although Rachel's face was distorted with disguise, she smiled sadly. Brin saw nothing but beauty.

"It is a story worthy of any ballad," Rachel said. "My dream is to find a love like theirs."

Again she forced Brin to wait. This time, however, he saw that she was collecting her thoughts, and he did not interrupt.

"I, of course, have read the letter," she said. "Before leaving Scotland, it was my task to set the letter to memory, for it was considered too dangerous to travel with it, and Edwin and I needed to be able to refer to it. Instead of answering your questions, then, with your permission I shall recite as surely as if I am reading from it."

"Please," Brin said softly. *It would be as if his father were speaking directly to him from beyond the grave.*

"This is the letter, then." Rachel closed her eyes and began to speak.

Father, we have been betrayed. By whom, I cannot say, although as I near death, I wish I had this knowledge to pass on. I only know the betrayer is one of us. Not only has my life been betrayed but the mission as well.

It happened thus. Upon crossing the mountains and reaching the plains of northern Italy, I was sent from our small party of travelers into a small town to seek provisions. Just outside of that town, I was waylaid and taken into the trees near a river. My attackers wore masks. They began to beat me senseless. I pretended early unconsciousness, hoping the beating would end. When it did, they began to search me. I heard one of them speak of the precious ring, which I had not taken with me but left behind safely hidden.

As you reach this portion of the letter, the same question will occur to you as it did to me. How is it that thieves could know of the ring? Or that they knew it was my responsibility to safeguard it?

Father, you know better than I do that those who expect us in Rome would never betray the cause or the existence of the ring. Even if one among them were so inclined, none there have knowledge of how we travel, when we are to arrive, or even how we look. It is impossible for them to know we have entered Italy. The source of betrayal, I concluded, could not be one among them but could only be one of those traveling with us.

Yet even as I concluded this, the knowledge appeared of little use because imminent death was upon me. The thieves bound my arms and legs and tossed me into the river. The current took and battered me. Downstream, around a bend, the river pushed me up against a boulder, and there, for a few moments, I was able to draw air.

I would have died except a woman was washing clothes on the bank. She waded out, and although the rushing water pushed higher than her waist, she persisted. She had a knife, which I found remarkable at the time, but later I discovered she was part of a gypsy camp. With that knife, she cut my bonds and helped me reach shore.

I was too weak and injured to move. This woman hid me and returned at night to tend to my wounds and to feed me. She kept my existence a secret from the other gypsies, for they are united against all outsiders. This continued for one week while the gypsies camped outside of the nearby town.

Her name is Maria. Our love grew. We found a church, and a priest married us before God. In so doing, however, we both became fugitives. I from the betrayer among us. She from her gypsy clan, who were furious that she had joined with an outsider. The stakes were even higher and their fury even greater than I had dreamed, for she had kept hidden from me her position among them. They considered her a princess and were determined to bring her back, determined to kill me.

As fugitives, however, we had a mission. The ring was still hidden among those traveling to Rome. I did not feel safe openly returning to them, for this would give the betrayer knowledge that I was still alive.

It took a month to find them. Then, at night, I went into the camp and took my horse away from them. I had hidden the ring in a hollowed out portion of my saddle. Maria and I fled.

Even with the ring in my possession, I did not consider it safe to proceed to Rome. Although I still did not know who it was, the betrayer would be waiting for me and could easily claim I was the betrayer—for to all appearances, it was I who had disappeared and then returned in the night to steal the ring.

Furthermore, a handful of gypsies were still in relentless pursuit of Maria and me.

We could not rest easy and spent months moving day by day to avoid capture until, without warning, the hand of Black Death struck me. And as I near death, I see no other course except to take the risk of writing this letter and praying it does not fall into the wrong hands.

I doubt I will live to the end of this week. It fills me with great sadness to leave Maria. Our love is a greater joy than I imagined any love could be. The joy and mystery of it surely reflects the love that God our Father has given us all.

Yet I know death is merely a painful heartbeat, taking me into the great light. With this hope through Christ, I know that when Maria leaves this world, I will be there waiting for her.

I face death without fear. Maria will return to the gypsy camp, taking with her this letter, the ring, and our child, which she carries in her womb. We have decided it is there among the gypsies that she will be best able to give birth.

I take satisfaction in knowing the one who betrayed the secret of the ring has no knowledge of Maria in my life. Because of this, it is not possible that anyone knows the location of the ring. It shall remain so until this letter reaches you.

It is Maria's greatest wish, and mine, that somehow she will find a way to travel to Scotland once the child is born. If the Lord grants us this, Maria will return the ring to you. I know without asking that you will treat her as an equal among the Keepers of the Grail.

Yet I have taken provisions to ensure this letter will reach you if she cannot. At the seal of this letter, I shall pledge half a year's wages to the person who brings this letter unopened to you. Know then, if this letter reaches you without Maria, you will find the ring among the gypsies.

Your faithful servant, Christopher.

I was glad to hear Rachel read the letter too. These events in Brin's life started to make a lot more sense for me. Of course, I didn't know what was ahead in Rome or who the betrayer had been or exactly why the ring was so important, but I was hopeful that our Father wanted me to stay with Brin until those questions were resolved.

Yet with all that Brin—and I—had learned from the letter, I also wished Brin would remember the one part of his father's last written words that showed the ultimate joy provided by a human's faith in the love of our Father.

Yet I know that death is merely a painful heartbeat, taking me into the great light. With this hope through Christ, I know that when Maria leaves this world, I will be there waiting for her.

Brin's father knew that the plague would take his life very soon after writing the letter. It was a horrible disease, and, unlike him, many others in his situation had used their last energy to shake their fists in anger at our Father.

At a time when some towns saw half the people taken by Black Death, most believed that an angry God was punishing them for their sins.

Certainly, looking back on the devastation that sent millions upon millions to early deaths, the plague seems senseless at best.

But that's only if you believe that death is the end and the worst thing that can happen to a human.

As an angel, I implore you to view your existence against eternity. Earthly death simply takes you into another and greater world than you can imagine.

It's not the first time you've faced a change of this magnitude either.

You can't remember, of course, your time in your mother's womb, but it was safe and warm. All of your needs were filled. The darkness around you was comforting. Your mother's movement soothed you, and you spent hours of each day in blissful sleep. When you woke, you would move, pushing your little legs and arms against the constriction that held you, totally unaware that your arms and legs were destined for much grander tasks.

Your first moments outside the safety of the womb. What a shock! What a strange and new universe! Instead of warm fluid surrounding you, there was the harshness of cold air. Strange noises. Bright lights that made no sense. And when the fluid drained from your lungs, you were forced into a totally new existence where you had to draw your own oxygen. You cried and kicked and wanted nothing more than the safety of the only world you had known, the place where you were bound so tightly that you couldn't even extend your arms or legs.

Yet within hours, you understood that the womb had been a prison. And as you grew and explored more of the world, you would never for a moment trade your freedom to be bound like that again.

On our side, in the presence of our Father and among those of you whose earthly faith in Him gave eternal life in His presence too, we all understand that the new freedom you gained by leaving your mother's womb is infinitely less than the freedom our Father offers to all humans after death.

When we are sent to watch over you, not a single angel spends an anxious moment thinking about whether you will die. Because we know it is inevitable that you are going to die. Our concern is whether you are prepared for eternity before it happens.

As for Brin, I could only hope he would find the faith that his father had. Nothing could be more important. Not even whatever was waiting for him in Rome...

16

When Rachel had finished reciting the letter, the sudden silence was as loud as a clap of hands, and it brought Brin back to the reality of the hillside where he sat beneath a tree.

Many thoughts went through Brin's mind, but he spoke only one. "It is not me you sought. You sought the ring."

She understood the slight bitterness of his tone.

"You are wrong," she said. "Yes, the ring is of great value. But your grandfather wishes very much to have you rejoin him in Scotland."

"Me? A gypsy mongrel he has never seen?"

She smiled. "You will be welcomed as royalty."

Brin's puzzlement was obvious.

"Your father wrote this letter to his own father," she said. "Your grandfather. Does that not mean anything to you?"

Brin's mind had been full of the bitter sweetness of hearing his father's last words. "I suppose," he said slowly, "it means he loved his father."

"You can have no doubt of that," Rachel said. "But think. The bearer of this letter was promised a half year's wages. Could a peasant farmer afford to pay this?"

"Perhaps not," Brin answered.

"The lord of the kingdom could afford it," Rachel said. "Your grandfather, who cherished you from the moment he knew of you. Do you not think, then, that part of our task, beyond finding the ring, was to bring you back to him?"

Brin turned his head away from her. It would not do for Rachel to see that he blinked away tears. He composed himself before speaking again.

"I have a home waiting for me?"

"Yes," she said gently.

The letter also clearly showed a trust his father had in God. Why? How? Brin wanted to know more. And he wanted to know more about this Christ. How could a man die and then rise again from the dead? Much as he wanted to discuss these matters, Brin was compelled to ask a different question. The obvious question.

"Who betrayed my father? Do you now know?"

"That is as much a mystery to us now as it was to your father."

"Could it be the same who betrayed Edwin? Who drugged and searched me at the tree?"

"I think it likely," she said. "Which is why we travel in disguise."

"The ring," he said after some reflection. "Tell me about it."

Rachel paused a moment before answering. Etched over her silence was the tittering of birds and the rustle of tall grass in the breeze.

"It is part of a map," she finally said. "And I can tell you no more until we reach Rome."

There was such firmness in her voice that he knew further questions would be of no use.

As if to keep him from pressing her, she stood. "Shall we go?"

He rose and followed her back to the road.

Christopher, he thought as he walked alongside her. *I now know my father's name. What a gift. Christopher.*

Brin's joyful mood lasted the entire day. He realized he had begun to trust Rachel. This too gave him joy. Rachel had brought him the knowledge he had wanted his entire life. Best of all, this knowledge was far better than he could have dreamed. His grandfather waited for him with love!

Brin's joy did not diminish as he fell asleep. They had stopped at a roadside inn, and Rachel had produced the coin needed for a meal and one night's lodging.

Alone on his straw bed, Brin smiled into the darkness, thinking about all he had learned. Sleep began to take him. The warmth of his joy was almost as comforting as a blanket.

I was born into a family of royalty, he thought for the hundredth time. *I have a home waiting for me.*

Life is a wonderful mystery, he told himself in his final moments before sleep.

Brin's joy did not last long. When he woke, it was to a sack over his head and rough hands turning him over.

17

A hand pressed against Brin's mouth before he could scream. His own arms were pinned against his side.

He fought and twisted. He kicked out to feel a satisfying thump. He heard a muffled curse.

A blow rang his ears. He shook off the pinpricks of white pain that lanced his eyes and twisted more. He lashed out with his feet, this time hitting nothing but air.

Another blow to his head. This one harder.

Brin guessed that two, maybe three people were holding him down on the cot. What chance did he have, fighting blind?

He stopped fighting.

Beneath the hood, mouth held tight, Brin panted for breath through flared nostrils, as much from fear as from his efforts.

Was this an execution? Would a dagger slice through his ribs next?

Brin waited for the burning slice of steel. Instead hands pushed against him.

He tried to make sense of what he could feel. Two pairs of hands held him down. Another pair searched the clothes he wore beneath the single blanket.

No words were spoken. Not from Brin, for the hand on his mouth was unwavering in pressure. Not from his attackers.

The search ended.

The hands, however, did not release him.

Brin strained to hear. It sounded as though one of the attackers was now searching the tiny room. The shuffling sounds continued until the searcher had gone through the room twice.

Brin heard a grunt. A grunt of disappointment?

"Nothing," came a harsh whisper. "It is not here."

"The straw then," came a whispered answer.

The hands pushed him onto the floor and held him there with great strength. Brin could imagine his attackers leaning down on him with the full force of all their weight.

He heard the third person rip apart the mattress. Then he heard the jingle of coin. They had found his small pouch of silver and gold.

The coins were scattered on the floor.

"Not among these," the harsh whisper announced. "Where can it be?"

"Enough," the answering voice whispered. "We have risked too much time in here."

The hands released him just as quickly as the attack had taken him from sleep. Quiet footsteps left the room.

Brin gasped for a mouthful of air, sucking the fabric of the hood against his face. He pulled it away and yanked the hood off his head.

Were it not for the hood, the light of a single candle set in a holder left on the floor, and the scattered coins visible in that soft light, Brin might have been tempted to believe he had just woken from a vivid nightmare.

He knew, of course, what the attackers sought.

The ring.

————————

Time passed until Brin found the strength to move. He rubbed his face, sick with the only conclusions he could draw.

They had traveled all day in the hot, heavy disguise of old, poor peasants. Who else could know they were here, then, but Rachel? Who else could have sent them into the room but her?

His betrayer was Rachel.

It was now obvious to Brin that she hadn't believed him when he said he did not have the ring.

He thought more. He decided she would not have been able to send these attackers into his room the night before at the monastery among the monks. This night, then, had been her first and best opportunity.

Brin gathered his scattered coins from the floor. His hands moved slowly, as if another person were scooping them into the leather pouch. His mind still fought questions.

Brin began to wonder if everything she had told him during the day was as false as her motives.

He did not wonder for long. He immediately told himself it was ridiculous to believe that he could be the grandson of a lord of a kingdom in a faraway land.

Rachel could just as easily have lied about his parents. As a gypsy accustomed to fleecing peasants, Brin knew the best lies were the ones that people desperately wanted to believe. Brin could think of no lie he would want to believe more than a wonderful tale about a mother and father who risked their lives for a great love.

Brin pondered all of this, growing more bitter and angry at Rachel as the night passed.

Then it occurred to Brin that his attackers had not killed him as he feared. He began to wonder about that too.

This ring must be of such great importance that they could not risk killing him until they knew for certain where the ring was. Or until he had sketched the symbols for them to read.

A map, Rachel had said.

A map to what?

All Brin needed to do was close his eyes to bring back all the symbols on both sides of the ring. He knew, though, it might be a letter of death to actually put these symbols into charcoal lines on paper. Once they had the ring or its symbols, his life had no value. It seemed, then, his greatest value was in the knowledge only he had.

If that were true, he decided, he must keep the knowledge to himself as long as possible.

Anger and bitterness gave him resolve.

Whatever this game was, he was determined to win. If the ring were the only weapon he had, he would use it. He would play along with Rachel, pretending he trusted her. When he finally discovered what treasure the map would bring, he would find a way to betray her in turn. And take the treasure.

With a grim smile, Brin piled the straw back into the shape of a mattress. If he wanted to win this game, he needed rest.

He blew out the candle and slid beneath his blanket.

He closed his eyes.

In the morning, he would gaze upon the innocent smile that she used to hide her treachery. He would smile back with equal innocence. And with equal treachery.

18

From the north, they traveled the Via Flaminia—the Flaminia Road—into Rome. Rachel was talking about history and drawing pictures with words so clearly that Brin could see the marching lines of Roman soldiers as they returned triumphant from the wars centuries earlier, hear their measured footsteps along the stones, and imagine the throngs of citizens and slaves cheering them on as they entered the city.

Before they reached the Tiber River, rolling hills of pasture and olive groves with occasional stone farmhouses were to be seen on both sides of the road. Once near the Seven Hills, however, buildings began to press upon them, as did a stream of travelers in carts and on foot, mule, and horse.

Brin and Rachel allowed themselves to be swept along with the confusion and bustle of the travelers. For Brin it was almost overwhelming. Much as he had heard about the great city, he never dreamed there could be so many people, so many great buildings.

He had long given up asking Rachel where they were going in Rome, so he remained silent, drinking in the sights and sounds and smells of a city of dust and stone in the midday heat.

On and on they pressed until Brin began to believe the city stretched forever. Through the markets. Into slums of buildings pushing in crooked lines against each other.

Then the road opened. Brin gaped from a distance as they passed the Palace of the Popes, yet Rachel did not allow him to stop.

She brought him past great ruins—columns of stone standing alone amidst rubble—then to a coliseum of such proportions that he believed her stories of men called gladiators who fought beasts or each other in the open arena before spectator crowds of thousands. He marveled with horror at other stories of believers of the man called Christ, cast before lions and bears to be killed for the amusement of those same spectators. Although Rachel had spent much of their travel talking about Christ, Brin still could not understand why men and women and children would choose such a death before giving up their beliefs in the Christ.

Brin began to notice they were now traveling against the stream of horses and mules and carts and stragglers instead of with it. Soon after, the buildings began to thin and the green of countryside became open once more.

Brin could not stop himself from asking. "Have we passed through Rome? Where are we going?"

She surprised him by answering without evasion.

"We are now on the Via Appia, the road that a man named Paul had taken into Rome as he brought the belief of Christ to the Romans."

Rachel pointed to the city wall behind them. "The outer limit of the ancient city," she explained. "Ahead, we walk as this road gently climbs the ridge. In three miles, we reach our destination."

"How can you be so sure?" If, finally, Rachel was prepared to speak of those things she had earlier remained silent about, he wanted to press her.

"Before I left Scotland," she said, "your grandfather taught me all that I should memorize as we moved through the city. He taught me how to find the place."

"And how did he know?"

"Many, many years earlier, he traveled the same road."

"Why?" Brin asked. "Is this where you finally explain about the Keepers of the Grail?"

"Can't you wait the half hour until we arrive?"

"Arrive where?" he asked, unable to count how many times earlier he had asked the same question.

"Now that we are so close," she said, "I see no harm in answering. Ahead, our guide waits for us at ancient burial grounds."

———

They stopped in a grove of olive trees just off the road.

"I am not tired," Brin said. "We need not rest on my account."

Rachel smiled. "My friend, we have arrived."

"Here?" Brin swept his arms to take in the trees, the small shrubs, the tall grass. "How can this be an ancient burial ground? Where is our guide?"

"Patience," she answered. "There, past the trees. That building is our destination."

It was midafternoon, just past the greatest heat of the day. Despite his irritation and curiosity, Brin was glad to be off the hot dusty road and in the shadows of the trees as they walked.

As they arrived at the small stone building, Brin snorted. How could this be a destination worth a week of travel in disguise as an old man? It was almost in ruins. Half of the clay tiles of the roof were gone, the other half crumbling. Where a door had once stood, there were only traces of rotted timber.

"Inside," she said. "There we wait."

"I do not understand."

"You will tonight," she said. "When our guide arrives. He will see the lit candles I place in the window and know that after all these years, the Keepers of the Grail have returned."

Rachel began to pull the wax disguise away from her face. She invited Brin to do the same. She removed her old outer clothes, as did he. Grateful to shed the weight and filth, Brin felt as if he had become a new person.

He looked at Rachel with a sideways glance. He fought a mixture of admiration and distrust. In the dappled shade from branches and leaves of a tree above the ruined building, she was a wonderful and unwanted distraction.

Rachel moved to a wall deepest in the shade and sat, leaning back against it.

Brin paced.

"The small lights of candles this deep among the trees will be impossible to notice this far back from the road," he said. "Only if someone has been watching will they even know we have entered here."

"I am certain we have been watched," she replied. She reached into the cloth sack she had been carrying for their provisions. She offered him water from a leather pouch, along with bread and cheese.

Brin, however, could not relax. Her serenity and certainty only agitated him more. "For a week, you tell me nothing," he said, an edge to his voice. "Then you promise an ancient burial ground and bring me instead to a ruined building. And now you want me to believe that someone has been watching and waiting. You want me to believe that day by day, year by year, this forgotten grove of olive trees outside of Rome has always been watched."

"Of course," she said. "A treasure as great as the one which waits below us is always guarded."

She gave him a smile. "Trust me, all we have to do is wait."

Trust her? Brin smiled back, hiding his thoughts. Never.

Angel Blog

There's probably something I should mention at this point. Something, um, important.

Remember earlier when I emphatically educated you about angels' wings? (The fact that we don't have them!)

There are other bad public relation myths about us too. Ones like buying good luck charms in the shape of an angel will give you divine protection. Or others that make us look like cute, cuddly cherubs. You could guess my response by now to those, couldn't you.

It's simple. We are spiritual beings. You are physical beings.

You are also physical beings who often don't want to believe there is a spiritual world. So you spend a lot of effort trying to, well, humanize us by putting us in make-believe forms that are physical. And harmless.

It's like you don't ever want to think about the, um, important thing I need to mention.

Let me put it this way. A while back—it doesn't seem long ago to me, of course—there was this mean commander of a big army. This commander, an Assyrian, threatened God's people in the land of Israel. This Assyrian commander had the luxury of 185,000 soldiers to back up his threats against the Israelites. Until he woke up in the morning to discover all of his soldiers were dead.

Stop and think about how many soldiers that is. At 30 to a school bus—yes, I know they didn't have school buses back then, but work with me on this—that would be nearly 6200 school buses filled with soldiers. If you still can't picture that, then realize that, bumper to bumper, all those school buses would form a line 35 miles long. There you have it, enough soldiers to fill a 35-mile line of school buses. Let me repeat, the Assyrian commander woke up to find all of them dead. D-E-A-D. As in not breathing, not moving, and certainly not capable of picking up swords and swinging them against the Israelites.

The gory details of how all 185,000 soldiers were killed are not the point here. This is the point: They were all killed by a single angel sent by our Father. In a single night.

Sure, we're guardians. Sure we're messengers. Those are the nice things you always choose to remember about angels.

We're also powerful enough to do *whatever* our Father asks of us. And we *always* do whatever our Father asks of us—even if the results mean a 35-mile line of school buses filled with dead ancient soldiers.

Our Father has a grand plan, you see. Do you think He would allow anyone or anything to get in the way of His plan? Think anyone or anything would be able to escape the powers He gives to His angels in order to see His plan accomplished?

And what if Brin—who had heard the gospel message repeatedly from Rachel—was going to choose the way of darkness?

I certainly didn't want that to happen.

But I was prepared.

Because if our Father finally revealed to me that I'd been sent not as a guardian in the way I wanted to assume, but instead to eventually stop Brin from acting against our Father, I would follow His orders, whatever they were, without hesitation....

19

Bells from the center of Rome penetrated the darkness. Brin counted. Ten times. The black velvet of a clear night had long since arrived, and the scattered white dust of stars showed through the gaps in the roof.

Rachel sat beneath the open window. Seven candles were lined across the window. The flames burned straight in the breezeless air. The candles themselves were nearly stubs. When they had first begun waiting, the candles had been new.

"Without more candles in your sack, you are sure to be disappointed," Brin said, standing again and stretching. "Or perhaps your guide is blind. If indeed he exists."

"Not blind," a voice said from behind him. "Merely silent and cautious."

Brin stumbled backward and spun around. Still he saw no one.

"Know that here lies united an army of saints." The voice came from beyond the open doorway, drifting in quietly.

"These venerable tombs enclose their bodies," Rachel recited, equally quietly and with no fear, "while the kingdom of heaven has already welcomed their souls."

Brin watched the opening carefully, waiting for a deeper blackness to show him that a person had moved into the doorway. Yet only the voice entered.

"Here lie the companions of Sixtus, who bear the trophies won from the enemy," came the voice. "Here lie the brotherhood of popes who guard the altar of Christ."

Rachel took a breath. "Here too I, Damasus, confess I would like to be buried were it not for the fear of disturbing the ashes of these holy persons."

Brin waited for the voice to return. It did not. Instead, seconds later, the flames of the candles were extinguished by someone outside the ruined building. Brin jumped and stumbled in the opposite direction.

"Come," the voice said as Brin was recovering himself. "Step outside."

"Fear not," Rachel said to Brin, standing. "He is our friend. And he knows we are his friends. I have replied as he expected. And he as I required. From an inscription on a tomb below."

"Tomb? Below?"

In the darkness, Brin felt her take his hand. He allowed her to take him outside. She dropped his hand.

The outline of the man in front of them was tall, the shoulders bowed.

Without a word, he began to walk away from them, his footsteps soft in the deep grass.

Rachel followed. Then Brin.

Fifty steps away he turned, directly into a hedge.

"Protect your face with your arms," he said. "Otherwise the branches will scratch your face."

Again Rachel followed with Brin behind, groping as a blind man in the deeper darkness of the branches. His hands found Rachel's shoulders. She reached up and squeezed his fingers.

Her shoulders dropped. Then Brin understood. They were walking down steps. Slowly. It did not take them long to reach the bottom. Only a slight creaking warned Brin that a door had been opened. The faint glow of a torch showed narrow tunnel walls.

The tall figure stepped inside. Rachel did not hesitate to do the same.

Brin paused. What madness was this? Entering the depths of the earth with the woman who had betrayed him twice already?

Rachel stepped back and found his hand again.

"You will not be met with harm," she said. "Give me your trust."

Trust was last of any possession he would grant her. Only his vow to return treachery with treachery gave him the courage to move ahead.

Once he was inside, the guide closed the door behind him.

All three walked toward the glow of the torch. As the light grew, Brin was able to see more of his surroundings. The tunnel was hardly higher than the guide's head. The tunnel walls were narrow; Brin could stretch his arms like wings, and his fingertips brushed both sides.

The tunnel turned once, and the light grew even brighter. They proceeded another dozen steps. In that short space, two other tunnels broke off in different directions.

Brin saw too that ledges had been cut into the tunnel walls. These ledges were about the length of a body, only a couple of feet high, and a couple of feet deep. Every few steps, three or four ledges appeared on each side, one ledge above the other and above the other. Some ledges were plastered over, contents hidden. Some were empty. Some contained wooden boxes. Others had shrouds, and, walking as quickly as he was to stay with them, Brin could not determine what the thin, ghostly cloth covered.

Brin remained silent and followed, unable to make sense of it.

The tunnel turned once more before they finally reached an open area, lit by the flames of the torch set into the wall.

For the first time, Brin clearly saw the guide. An old priest in simple black garb.

"Greetings from the Keepers in Scotland," Rachel said, stepping forward and formally embracing the man. "And greetings from my brother Edwin, who was unable to travel with us. My own name is Rachel. This is Brin."

"Greetings and welcome," the guide said. "My name is Julius. After all these years, welcome to the hidden catacombs of St. Callixtus."

"Catacombs?" asked Brin.

"Yes," the guide said. "Burial chambers for the followers of Christ during the time of the great empire. Here, in 20 miles of tunnels, and forgotten over the last four centuries, are the remains of over a half million dead."

20

Brin shuddered. The ledges dug into the walls made sudden sense to Brin. *Bodies.* That's what had been on the ledges.

The guide frowned. Brin could see him closer now. The man's face was thin and bearded with gray.

"I was told to expect a young woman," Julius said. He turned to Rachel and spoke hardly above a whisper. "And of course, Edwin, whom I would have recognized. I am sad to hear he was not able to join you. The presence of a third person, however, is a surprise. As is his question. How is it he does not know of the catacombs? Is he not one of us?"

"I wish that he were," Rachel said. "But that is a matter for his grandfather in Scotland to decide. As for now, we need him greatly."

Julius nodded gravely. It impressed Brin that Julius did not express doubt in Rachel's answer. Rachel was far younger than he, and a stranger. Keepers of the Grail, Brin decided, respect each other greatly, regardless of station in life.

"It was Brin's father," Rachel explained further to Julius, "who first began the journey here with the ring you need. When he disappeared, we believed him lost all these years. And then the letter arrived…"

Rachel explained the rest. The air in the tunnels was still and cool. The soft glow of the torch light showed there was beauty even in the shadows of her face. Brin watched and listened, captivated by her presence and outraged at her calm lies.

He wanted to tell Julius that Rachel was the betrayer, seeking the ring for herself. But Brin knew patience would pay greater rewards. He listened as she finished the story.

"So you and Edwin spent the better part of a year in the north, searching the gypsy clans for word of a fair-haired gypsy," Julius said. "And you have found him, along with the ring given him by his father, Christopher, may his soul rest in peace."

"Brin does not have the ring," Rachel said. "He cast it away, so that it would not fall into the hands of those who attacked my brother."

Julius let his shoulders slump. "Surely you know all of this is for nothing without the second ring. Mile after mile of these tunnels wind beneath the city. There are four levels. Not even I, who have spent my whole life searching these tunnels, know them all. Daily, I must walk with pieces of chalk in my pockets, marking the walls where I have been so that even I will not get lost. How can we find the treasure without the second ring?"

"He will sketch it for us," Rachel said. "He knows the symbols by heart."

Julius shook his head. "Did his grandfather not explain before you left Scotland? It is not sufficient merely to find where the jewels of Callixtus are hidden, but the rings themselves serve as keys. There are two slots in the wall, one for each ring. Once both rings are inserted, it springs a lock, and the hidden door opens."

Jewels of Callixtus? Brin felt his heart beat faster.

"I do understand," Rachel said. "It was explained to me very clearly. The ancients devised a cunning system to keep the treasure from thieves. Supports behind the walls will collapse if the door is not opened on its hinges. We cannot dig to get the jewels, for not only will they be lost, but the entire portion of the tunnel will fall on us."

"This, then, is the reason for my despair," Julius said.

"Edwin and I have given our problem much thought," she said, removing the sack she had slung over her shoulder. "Before we left Edwin behind at the monastery to recover from his wounds, he suggested a solution. All it requires is a Keeper's bag of tricks."

Brin knew this was the sack which contained her exploding powder, the blinding acid, and sleeping potion for darts. He would not be surprised at anything she pulled from it. Except for what appeared in her hands.

It was merely a lump of wax.

"Julius," she said. "Here is our second ring."

Julius steepled his fingers and regarded her thoughtfully.

"Once we find the location, we melt this wax and pour it into the slot. After it cools, we gently pull the wax free. It should hold the shape of the ring. From it, we make a mold. From the mold, we form another ring."

"It may suffice," Julius said. "It just may suffice! In the early days, thieves would not have had the time that you and I have. Yes, it may take several days for us to make a new ring, but now centuries later the tunnels are ours alone."

Both turned to Brin.

"All we need," Rachel said to Brin, "is your sketch. Julius has the other ring. With it, we can move through this maze to the jewels of Callixtus."

"Yes," Julius said. He could not hide his excitement. "Perhaps even within the hour. Sketch it on the dirt of this floor, and Rachel and I shall proceed."

"No," Brin said. "You will not proceed without me. Furthermore, explain what it is we seek. How it happens to be there. And how my grandfather knew of it."

"Young man," Julius began. "Words mean so little against what is the prize of centuries, and against what will greatly assist the Keepers of the Grail over the next centuries."

Rachel sighed. "Julius, I am afraid he is more stubborn than a team of mules. I know him well enough to recognize that when he speaks in such a tone, he cannot be budged."

Then I will tell you," Julius said with a sigh louder than Rachel's, "about the catacombs and the jewels of Callixtus."

21

"It began during the first century after Christ's death," Julius said in gentle, modulated tones. "After the apostle Paul reached Rome with his message of hope, a growing number of slaves and citizens began to convert to faith in a risen Lord. Most were buried in common cemeteries, among nonbelievers. By the second century, rich families of converts made room on their estates for the burial of poorer Christians. Excavations began then, for the rocky ground of these estates—vineyards and olive groves—consist of soil over top of tufa. They…"

Julius had been watching Brin closely, for he saw his puzzled expression.

"Tufa," Julias said, "is volcanic rock. Soft and easy to dig. It hardens once exposed to air. If you look closely at these walls, you can see the marks of the workers' picks."

He allowed Brin the chance to examine the walls by torch-light before continuing.

"The workers removed this rock and dirt by basket. You have already seen the ledges they carved to make room for bodies."

Brin nodded.

"There are many catacombs in Rome," Julius said. "These, the catacombs of St. Callixtus, are among the largest. From the third century on, the Church of Rome administered these tombs, and for many years a deacon named Callixtus was the custo-dian."

Julius walked several steps. Brin merely watched.

"Come with me," Julius said, growing more enthusiastic as teacher. He took the torch from the wall. "Your eyes will teach you better than your ears."

Brin followed first this time, with Rachel behind.

Julius led them farther down the tunnel until they reached another opening, much larger than where they had first stopped. He swept the torch to let Brin see the full extent of the widened walls.

"The Crypt of the Popes," Julius whispered. "We do not wor-ship the popes as saints; however, they were men of God and deserve much respect. Antherus, Fabian, Lucius, Eutichian. And Damasus."

Torchlight showed an arched roof of brick with marble columns supporting the roof. There was an altar. In front of it stood a table, made of a large sheet of smooth marble covered with an inscription.

"Go ahead," Julius invited Brin. "Step forward. Read the inscription. It is the one you heard Rachel and I recite to each other. Translated from the Latin, of course."

Brin squirmed. He did not want to admit that he had no knowledge of Latin, let alone that he could not read.

"He has already heard it," Rachel said with a light laugh. "Let us not waste his time by straining his eyes in this poor light."

"My apologies," Julius said with a slight bow.

For a moment, Brin was tempted to throw aside all his bitterness toward Rachel. She had been gracious, preserving him from embarrassment.

"The Christians worshiped here," Rachel said quickly to keep the silence from becoming awkward. "Not only did the catacombs serve as a burial place, but also as a church, for there were times the Roman emperors persecuted the Christians."

"Yes, Rachel," Julius said, "whoever taught you, taught you well. Christians worshiped here and used it as a place of refuge during those difficult times. Imagine how cruel the Romans could be. Covering Christians with tar and hanging them on a post before lighting them so they would be human torches."

Again, Brin found himself wondering about the determination of people who would rather cling to their beliefs than save their lives.

"Why kill them?" Brin asked. "Rachel told me that the Romans encouraged different beliefs and customs."

"Ah, yes," Julius said with the enthusiasm of one who enjoyed debate but has not had the chance for some time. "But once it began to take root, there were some emperors who found these new beliefs threatening."

"They are only beliefs," Brin protested.

"Beliefs much different than the religions tolerated by the Roman emperors," Julius countered. "The other religions compromised and adapted themselves to the whims of officials. The other religions were simply private affairs, serving the inner needs of those who selfishly preferred vague spiritual pronouncements."

Julius stopped and raised his forefinger as if addressing an assembly. "But Christ's message was much different. It was radical and rejected the cults of the emperors, bringing a total renewal to each believer and, in so doing, threatened to change society."

Julius took a breath. "You see, it was revolutionary to preach that every man, even a slave, is brother to the other, and that we are all children of God."

He gasped with mock horror. "Imagine! Preaching that we should help the poor. Preaching that all men should love all men as a reflection of God's love for us. Then actually acting upon it!"

Despite his suspicions, Brin could not help but be entranced by Julius. His manner had changed from a stooped old man to one flushed with energy. If this was how Keepers learned, Brin would enjoy the chance to become one of them and...

He shut his mind to the thought. No, Brin had already decided his action against Rachel and those she represented.

"More revolutionary," Julius was saying, "these followers of Christ taught His message that the poor should not be abused and that justice must be the goal of those in power. How could an emperor with a hardened heart and wealth built upon the backs of thousands of slaves tolerate such a belief?"

Julius resumed walking. As they entered the narrow tunnels again, he pointed from side to side, from ledge to ledge. "All these buried here were welcomed during their lives by other Christians. Rich or poor, ugly or beautiful, they were all loved. In life, then, they found freedom. And here…"

Julius paused again. "Here in death they found freedom to be buried as they wished. The Romans preferred cremation, but the Christians did not. Over the centuries, they all found refuge here as a place of rest for the bodies they left behind as they journeyed to heaven."

"Heaven," Brin whispered, more to himself than to be heard.

"Heaven," Rachel whispered, closer behind him than he had expected. "Where God the Father waits with love as surely as your grandfather waits for you in Scotland. With open arms. And love that does not depend on what you have done, but simply on the fact that you are. And Brin, heaven is much, much lovelier than any home on earth. You will be treated as royalty in both places."

Inside, he shook off her words. She was a snake of treachery. Outwardly, however, he nodded with a smile.

Julius had gained a few steps on them in the narrow tunnel.

"This is a delight," Julius said over his shoulder. "I have been the sole custodian of these catacombs for so long, it is wonderful to be able to speak of them."

"They are secret?" Brin asked, following.

"Only because they have been forgotten," Julius answered. "The empire fell and by the eighth century, the popes were unable to provide protection for the relics in the catacombs. Gradually, the relics were moved to churches in the city, for the Christian faith had triumphed to become the accepted faith. The catacombs were no longer needed now that churches served all. Within decades, landslides and vegetation covered most of the entrances to these catacombs. Two hundred years later, no traces of them existed to the world above."

"Except to Keepers of the Grail?" Brin asked. They had nearly reached the first opening where Julius had gathered them before the torch.

"Yes," Julius said, "except to Keepers of the Grail."

He glanced nervously at Rachel. "How much does he know?"

"Some," she said, "but not all."

"Explain it all," Brin said. "You've said little about the Keepers of the Grail. Unless I hear the rest of the answers, I will not draw the map."

Julius nodded assent.

"Brin," Rachel said, "when you become one of us, you will learn our complete history, which began centuries ago when the Knights Templar were formed to protect Christian pilgrims who visited the Holy Land. The first knights relied on donations to survive, but within 200 years this order was so powerful they could defy all but the pope himself."

"You are Keepers of the Grail," Brin said quietly. "Not Knights Templar."

"Patience," Julius murmured.

Rachel smiled gently. "He has been very patient so far."

Again, Brin fought any feeling of trust for Rachel.

"Keepers of the Grail," he said.

"The Templars," she continued, "accumulated such great landholdings and wealth that less than 60 years ago, Philip the Fair, king of France, had all Templars arrested on grounds of heresy against God, because this was the only charge that would allow their money to be seized. Members of the Knights Templar were tortured to make ridiculous confessions, then killed."

"He would be aware of all of this," Julius said. "Don't speak to him as if he were a child."

"He was raised by gypsies," Rachel said. "Gypsies avoid authorities. And politics."

"Sorry," Julius whispered.

"Keepers of the Grail," Brin persisted. He was not going to let their discussion distract him.

"The Knights Templar as an organization was destroyed, and its wealth looted," Rachel said. "At least officially."

She dropped her voice. "Good men of faith are still banded together to fulfill the original vows of the Knights Templar—to help the poor as they pilgrim to Christ. Peasants have long stopped trying to visit the Holy Land, but they still reach for faith in God."

"And the wealth?" Brin said, thinking of the ring and their quest here in the catacombs. "Some of it still secretly exists? Like the jewels of Callixtus?"

"Not for the Knights Templar," Rachel said. "But for a group secret even within the secrecy of the Templar."

"Keepers of the Grail," Brin said.

Rachel and Julius nodded.

"The first vow of the Keepers is to protect the Grail, but some say it was lost centuries ago. Others say that in every generation there is one man within the Keepers who knows its location and passes it on to another before he dies."

"There is another vow?"

"Yes," Rachel answered Brin. "It is the reason that Julius here has remained to guard the catacombs."

"And the jewels of Callixtus," Brin said.

"And the jewels of Callixtus," she agreed. "Callixtus himself was an honorable man. Much in gold and jewels was donated to the cause of the faith, not only from those rich believers buried here, but from all Christians. Can you imagine how much wealth might be here from a half million believers? Legend says it is enough to buy a kingdom. Maybe two. Callixtus hid these riches during the times of persecution—"

"Here in the catacombs," Brin interrupted.

"Yes," Rachel said, not at all irritated. "Callixtus devised the map of the two rings. He also brought in craftsmen to build the hidden crypt and the invisible door which needed those two rings as a key, knowing that the miles of tunnel would make it impossible for them to ever find it again."

Brin nodded. Already he had lost all sense of direction, and they had barely penetrated any of the maze.

"Knowledge of the jewels of the crypt of Callixtus has always been passed from generation to generation among the Keepers of the Grail, but it was almost considered fanciful legend, even here in Rome where the Keepers have always had one of the rings safely guarded. Then your grandfather found the other ring in hidden tunnels beneath his castle, with a decayed parchment directing the finder to the catacombs here in Rome."

"And he sent my father, his son, with that ring."

"Yes," Rachel said. "Your grandfather was too old to travel to Rome himself, although in his younger days he had been here to visit other Keepers. You already know the remainder of it. Now do you understand why your ring had such great value?"

"But I don't understand who else would have known of it to be able to betray my father." Although Brin was sure that Rachel was the treacherous one of this generation, it did not explain who it had been all those years earlier when his father had traveled to Italy to die in the arms of the woman he loved.

"Within the Templar are others," Rachel whispered. "Darkness to our light. Among us, they still exist. Hidden, even to us who hide among the Templars."

Brin tried to absorb what he had learned.

Julius shook Brin's shoulder, gently. He handed Brin a dagger.

"Now, my son," Julius said. "If we have satisfied your curiosity, will you sketch in the earth here what you remember of both sides of the ring?"

He reached into his pocket and pulled forth a ring, similar in size to the one Brin's parents had left him.

"Adding the symbols on my ring will give us a map," Julius said. "I know the tunnels well enough that if your rendering is accurate, I have confidence we will find the hidden crypt."

Brin did not reply but knelt, placing his knees squarely on the ground. With the tip of the dagger, he began to scratch patterns in the packed dirt.

Half an hour later, they stood in front of the crypt of the jewels of St. Callixtus, deep within the earth.

But without the second ring, they could not open it.

Angel Blog

You probably think, as your self-appointed moral guide and guardian, that this is a great opportunity for me to point out that money is evil.

Yes, you're right. This is a good opportunity. The wealth of two kingdoms was sealed in that crypt. Already Brin's father had been betrayed for it. And now someone was trying to do the same to Brin. Great time for a lecture.

No, you're wrong. Despite this excellent opportunity, I can't tell you that money is evil.

I've seen it used to build hospitals. Schools. Send aid halfway across the world. Money feeds and clothes families, gives them a house. Money is very important, and at times, even wonderful.

But the love of money, that's a different story.

Your apostle Paul said it best: *For the love of money is the root of all kinds of evil. And some people, craving money, have wandered from the faith and pierced themselves with many sorrows.*

We angels are not blind to the price that too many humans pay for their money. Fathers working 80-90 hours a week, ignoring their families. Lying, cheating, stealing. Some of you hoard money when, if used properly, it could do so much good in the world.

In a way, we angels find this tragically amusing. We understand that your life on earth is so very, very short. Does it really help you to die with millions in a bank account while leaving behind wreckage in the lives of those you should have given more time and love?

Since I've been giving so much advice already, a little more won't hurt, right?

Stop asking yourself how much money things will cost you.

Ask instead how much your money will cost.

Down in the catacombs, when Brin followed Rachel and Julius away from the wealth of two kingdoms hidden in the tomb and back up to the olive grove, I hoped very much it wouldn't cost him his life.

And worse, his soul.

22

Hours later, Brin woke in the room that Julius had provided him in a small house near a church beyond the olive grove. He and the priest shared one room. Rachel had another.

After finding the crypt on the second level, it had taken less than half an hour for Julius and Rachel to make a mold by pouring melted wax into the opening for the missing ring. Once the wax had dried and they had taken the impression of the ring, the return trip to the surface had been a short 20 minutes of triumph and hope in the eerie quiet of the catacomb tunnels.

During that time, Brin had watched Julius carefully, making observations and marking them in his mind. When they reached the small house, Brin had drunk three cups of water before lying down to sleep.

It was no accident, then, that Brin woke during the stillest, darkest part of the night. He'd known the urgency of a full bladder would take him from sleep at the hour he needed.

On waking, Brin remained on his straw mattress. He did not move until he was satisfied Julius was in deep sleep. The priest snored with such enthusiasm, Brin immediately decided there was little fear the old man would wake.

Brin crept out from beneath his blanket. During all the time Brin had watched Julius, the priest had been careless only for a moment, while Brin had pretended sleep. Because of that, Brin knew where to search.

He squatted beside the wall at the foot of the priest's bed, alert for any movement from the old man. With slow steady movements of his hands, Brin felt along the wall and pried loose a stone which covered a hiding hole. Brin removed what he needed and set the stone back into place. Brin, after all, was a gypsy who had been trained his entire life to be an expert thief.

Still silent, and with his bladder now aching, Brin stepped from the room.

He had no intention of leaving the house, however. He groped along the walls to find the entrance to Rachel's room.

He listened carefully to the rhythm of her breathing. It did not alter as he entered her room. She had placed her sack—the one that held the tricks and potions—on the floor beneath the window. Brin lifted the sack, stepped back out of her room, and finally out of the house itself.

A half moon gave little light, but with it Brin was able to find what he sought in the depths of her sack.

Brin set aside what he needed. On his toes and alert for any sounds, he returned to the inside of the tiny house. As carefully as he had taken the sack, he returned it to where Rachel had left it on the floor.

Rachel's breathing had not changed. Briefly Brin thought of Rachel's happiness at finding the crypt of St. Callixtus. Remembering the peace and beauty in her smile softened his heart. He wondered if he should continue with his course of action.

As his determination wavered, Brin forced himself to also remember the sack over his head at the inn and the hands which had roughly searched him. Only by reminding himself of her treachery did he keep his resolve.

He stepped outside of her room.

He stopped to listen again to her breathing. No matter how skilled an actress she might be, there would be some change in the rhythm—slight or not—if she woke. Brin knew this, for many were the nights he had stolen away from the gypsies to be alone beneath the stars.

He heard only the continued softness of her deep breaths.

Finally he allowed himself to think of his bladder.

He stepped outside again, pressing himself against the front of the house to keep the pale light of the half moon from casting any shadow.

When he reached a tree almost against the house, he moved beneath it. From there, he crept farther away from the house.

Once he believed himself safe from detection, he walked through grass wet with dew to the next tree.

First matters first, he told himself. Hidden from the house, he emptied his bladder behind a tree.

From there, he made a direct line toward the olive grove.

Brin felt no fear moving through the deep shadows. Night, after all, was an old friend. And there was plenty of night left. With satisfaction, he judged that far more night remained than what he needed before an equally stealthy return to the house and to the two who slept inside, unaware of his departure.

23

Julius spent the entire next day in Rome, returning just before sunset. He found Brin and Rachel sitting beneath an olive tree, where they had almost finished a simple meal of chicken, soft bread, and the juice of pressed apples.

"The silversmith did just as you suggested, Rachel," Julius said. "First, he molded a clay ball around the wax impression, leaving a small hole. When the clay had dried sufficiently— which was an insufferable wait—he slowly heated the ball in an oven, until all the wax ran out the small hole. Then he poured molten silver through that hole into the clay mold. When the silver cooled, he cracked the mold open. And look!"

Julius opened his hand to show gleaming silver. The ring. An exact copy of the one which Brin had been given so many years earlier by his father.

He leaned over and handed it to Rachel. "Carry it for us."

She clenched it in her fist and then stood and briefly hugged the priest. Stepping back, she said, "Surely it will fit the opening, just as the wax did. Yet unlike wax, the pressure of hard silver will be enough to open the lock."

Julius nodded. "I see no reason to delay. What ceremony have we to fulfill? None. The jewels have been sitting in the dust of centuries. This very hour we shall begin to polish them."

"And divide them among us too?" Brin asked, still sitting.

Julius smiled indulgently. "I know you can hardly believe our intentions for all this wealth. But as we told you last night, half will remain here for the Keepers of the Grail. And half will be used to help the poor in places where the Knights Templar know there is need."

Rachel tugged at his hand. "Come, rise. I am as eager as Julius to open the crypt."

Brin stood and dusted his lap of bread crumbs. "You are certain you want me to join you? After all, you now have what you sought from me. The ring."

Through treachery, he nearly added.

"Brin," Rachel said, "I can think of nothing I want more than you by my side."

She blushed as the meaning of her words struck them both. "That is…" she stuttered, "as we return to the catacombs and open the crypt."

Julius chuckled. "Young man, it seems to me that you have a beautiful girl who regards you as more than a friend."

"Hush," she said to Julius. But she did not hide her smile for Brin.

Brin felt only confusion. Rachel had the ring now. What more could she gain by acting in this manner?

Unless, he decided, she meant further treachery in the depths of the catacombs. After all, with the bodies of a half million lost in the dark tunnels, what difference would one or two more make? If she wanted the wealth, with Brin dead, and perhaps Julius too, the jewels would be hers. And the secret of her treachery would never leave the catacombs.

Brin smiled and hid his thoughts. Then he spoke truth.

"Rachel," he said, "I too can think of nothing better than standing at your side as we open the crypt."

24

They retraced their steps from the night before. Through the olive grove to a thick hedge, down hidden steps cut into rock, to a small door. Inside, a slow-burning torch waited them.

Brin followed Julius and Rachel. He was determined to remain behind her. A dagger in the back was not how he wanted to die.

The torch showed small white *x*s on the tunnel walls. Julius had marked the path to the jewels the night before.

Brin would have preferred to walk with his eyes closed. Occasionally, one of the ledges would be open, the result of plaster falling away over time. Where there was no coffin, there would be heaped bones, ghostly soft in the light of the torch, with strands of hair shining near the skull. Century after century the remains of these bodies had lain undisturbed, long since clean of any decay.

Brin did not like these reminders of mortality, of death. Much as Rachel had spoken to him of heaven, much as she had explained to him that Christ was the Son of God and had lived among men to give them a home in heaven, Brin was not inclined to share her faith and hope in life beyond death. Her witness of Christ, after all, had little significance when she used a pretense of devout goodness to hide the core of treachery.

No, Brin preferred gypsies to her hypocrisy. Theft was a way of life for them, one into which he'd been raised. At least with them there was consistency. If one of them had attempted to steal the ring from Brin, he would have had only himself to blame. After all, around wolves, a man took steps to protect his sheep. But when a man began to believe the wolf was instead a friendly dog, only hollow bitterness resulted when the sheep were attacked.

Brin remained deep within his brooding thoughts as the three walked in silence, only the scuffling of their footsteps echoing in the tunnels. It gave him a dark satisfaction to think that he might return to her the treachery she had given him.

They followed the white chalk marks, easily visible, through turn after turn after turn. Fifteen minutes later, they arrived at another wide opening.

It was no more than five steps wide and five steps deep. Two other tunnels led away from the opening, so it appeared to be hardly more than a junction. There was a flat wall, free of ledges, between those two tunnels, barely wider than a man's shoulders.

This section was different from any other section of wall in the entire 20 miles of twisting, confusing maze. The sign of the cross had been scratched waist high into the soft lava rock. This cross was hardly bigger than the length of a thumb and impossible to see unless a person knew exactly where to look.

Directly above the cross, just below the roof of the tunnel, were two tiny slots. They were so close together that both could be touched with one hand of a person standing below and reaching upward. Again, unless a person knew *exactly* where to look, they were invisible. Indeed, the night before it had taken Julius ten minutes of searching to find them.

"I am almost afraid," Julius said when they stopped. "For all my brave talk about needing to fulfill no ceremony, it seems that after all these centuries, perhaps something of importance should happen before we test the hidden lock."

"Not a ceremony," Rachel suggested quietly, "but prayer. I can think of no better place or time."

Julius nodded.

Along with the other two, Brin bowed his head and joined hands.

As Rachel opened her heart in whispered words, Brin let his mind wander. He felt no guilt over this. The God she spoke to was not his God.

He thought of the afternoon she had wiped his face with a damp cloth, pretending concern that someone had used a potion to cause him to sleep beneath the tree. Had she expected her beauty to blind him? Did she think he would not realize she had directed him to the tree and that no other person would have known he would be there?

He thought of the morning after his head had been put into a sack and he had been searched for the ring. Across their breakfast, she had smiled innocently and asked him if he had slept well. As if he didn't know she had sent the ruffians into his room.

He thought of all the times during their days of travel that she had spoken to him of tales of the man called Jesus, telling him of miracles and of love and compassion and of a man risen from the dead.

He thought of how he had smiled and nodded during those hours, enjoying the tales as entertainment but refusing for a moment to believe her further in anything she said.

All this ran through Brin's mind as she prayed.

And one more thing. He had darts in his pocket, along with the tiny tube that gave him the power to propel those darts. Taken from her sack. The weapons of the Keepers were ready to be used against them.

Now if she tried to betray him once more by attempting to kill him here in the catacombs, he was prepared.

Rachel finished her prayer.

All three raised their heads.

And found themselves not alone.

"Edwin!" Rachel gasped.

Her brother stood nearby, watching them with a cruel smile beneath his red beard. He wore a cloak over fine clothes. In his right hand, he held a huge broadsword.

He bowed. "No less than I."

"But you...the monastery...how..." She could not find words.

"My dear sister," he said. "I was not hurt at all. It simply served me well for it to appear as such to the world."

In a flash, Brin understood how stupid he had been. He began to withdraw his hand from his pocket. If somehow he could bring his hand to his mouth and fire one of the darts already in the tube...

"Tut, tut," Edwin said to him. Edwin raised the broadsword and pressed the point of it against Rachel's neck. "I would prefer you all remained as motionless as stone."

"But Edwin!" she said.

"Don't prove to be tiresome," he told her. "Haven't you realized it by now? I am here to claim for me what St. Callixtus left behind centuries ago."

25

"You are the betrayer," Rachel said evenly. "The one that Brin's father described in his letter."

"Edwin was here on the earlier journey," Julius confirmed. "Years later, it is he who attempts it again."

Edwin snorted. "Why else did I arrange to have it appear that I had been attacked on the bridge when I first met with this gypsy? I could not merely rob him of the ring myself. No, I needed to cast suspicion elsewhere."

Brin gritted his teeth. The tube and the dart with the sleeping potion was no more than a quick movement away from his mouth. Yet if Edwin's sword pressed any harder against Rachel's throat, it would draw blood.

"Just like years before when I sought the ring from Christopher," Edwin said. "I hired strangers to be thieves. With no knowledge of why I wanted the ring or of its worth, a piece of gold was all it took. Only on this occasion, I hired them to rob me and the gypsy together."

He spat. "The mongrel outwitted them. I needed to promise them more gold to help me further."

"It was your idea that I go to Brin," Rachel said, hardly above a whisper. "Your idea that Brin give them a similar ring to fool them. Yet all along you were their master?"

"Brilliant, was it not? It was one more way to ensure you did not suspect me. While the monks were in prayer that day, I stole away from the monastery and found the gypsy by the tree, according to the instructions I had given you to give him. There I first searched him while the sleeping potion kept him unaware. When I did not find the ring, I concluded he had hidden it nearby, which did not bother me. I needed only to continue to play the role of an injured man at the monastery. After you both departed from the monastery, I stayed but a half day. It allowed me to follow you, unsuspected."

"It was you," Brin said, "you who sent the men into my room the night in the inn."

"No less."

"The night in the inn?" Rachel asked Edwin.

"I was searched again," Brin said to her. "I thought *you* were the betrayer. I thought you knew of the search and were hiding it from me. I am truly sorry I did not trust you."

Edwin laughed. "What pathos. This amuses me." He laughed again. "Yes, Rachel, my young and innocent sister. That night at the inn, the hired strangers helped me thoroughly search the gypsy and his possessions. It would have been much simpler to have the ring. I would have easily arrived in Rome long before you and found a way to take the other ring from Julius. When I knew the gypsy truly did not have the ring, I simply went ahead to Rome and waited for you. It had been my own suggestion, after all, that the gypsy sketch the ring's symbols. I knew one way or the other that you would lead me to this crypt. After Julius departed the silversmith today, a small bribe gave me what I needed to know. A ring had been cast. All I had to do was follow."

Julius had begun to edge away. Edwin pressed the sword harder into Rachel's throat, and she sucked in a breath of pain.

"Don't move, old man," Edwin said. "I'm rather enjoying all of this. You can all admire my clever deceptions."

An alarming thought hit Brin. Edwin would not be in this mood to boast unless he had already decided none of the three of them would ever leave the catacombs.

"Someone among the gypsies betrayed me?" Brin asked. Any time he could steal was precious if Edwin meant to kill them.

"The one named Marcel. I believe he was jealous of you. He was strong, he said, but you were quicker and smarter, and he hoped you would die."

It had never occurred to Brin that anyone would think that highly of him. In a strange way, it made him feel good that someone like Marcel had felt the need to throw harm his way.

"Evil has blinded you, Edwin," Julius said. "But it is not too late to turn back. God forgave Moses, David, and Paul. The three greatest men of the Bible, all murderers who were taken back into the fold of believers. If God can forgive them…"

Edwin's face twisted with hate. "Shut your mouth, old man."

"I cannot. Surely your soul is worth more than any wealth."

"Give me your ring, Julius, before I drain her life's blood."

Slowly, with shaking hands, Julius reached over and placed the ring in Edwin's free hand.

"You have my thanks," Edwin said.

Without warning, Edwin stepped sideways. He flicked his wrist to turn the blade outward, and with the swiftness of lightning hit a hammer blow against Julius' skull with the butt of the handle of his sword.

The thud of metal against bone sickened Brin.

Julius fell backward from the force of the blow. Brin's hands shot out to catch Julius as he toppled. Brin staggered backward to hold the man's weight.

"Drop him," Edwin commanded Brin.

Brin eased the old man to the ground. He heard strained breathing from Julius. The blow had not killed him.

"Troublesome mongrel," Edwin growled. "I told you to drop him. I expect you to obey me."

Edwin brought his sword back.

Brin had nothing to help defend himself against the heavy steel edge. When he'd reached for Julius, the tube and dart had fallen from his hand to be lost in the darkness of the tunnels.

Edwin advanced. The sword swooped with a sideways slash.

Brin jumped back, sucking his stomach as deep as he could. The edge of the sword ripped his shirt. But Brin could move back no farther. The tunnel wall pressed on him.

Edwin brought the sword back again, ready to kill Brin.

Angel Blog

Was this my moment? The reason I'd been sent into Brin's life since he was a baby?

I would not have been surprised if our Father sent me into their presence so all could see me. Sometimes that's all it takes. The sight of an angel, the shimmering light, the sense of a powerful supernatural presence that, for a moment, takes them to the borderline between the physical and spiritual worlds. After it has happened, many deny our existence for the rest of their lives, choosing to believe that their minds tricked them. Others, however, who trust in our Father, marvel at the memory again and again, even to their deathbeds, and we rejoice to finally meet them on our side of the border.

Nor would I have been surprised if our Father had chosen to intervene with an earthly phenomenon, like an earthquake. Or, had we been outdoors, a strike of lightning and clash of thunder. Doubters would call it coincidence, and believers would hold to the knowledge it was divine intervention.

Would I be called to intervene?

Would our Father unleash His power in the form of an earthquake? And if He did, would it be my mission to protect Brin from the tons of rock that would crumble around him?

I waited. With our Father, a day is like a thousand years, and a thousand years is like a day. Less than a heartbeat would have passed for Brin; to me, it was as if time stood still.

Then, in my trust of our Father's plan for Brin, I understood.

Brin had not yet made his choice. The fate of his soul was far more important than anything else that moment in the catacombs. More important than any temporary triumph the evil one would secure if Edwin killed Brin and escaped with the jewels. More important than the lives of Rachel and Julius, who had long since chosen the destiny that would take them to our Father when they crossed to our side.

This then, was not my moment.

I simply watched.

26

"No," Rachel told Edwin, her voice another weapon of steel. Edwin glanced back at her.

She held the shiny ring between her thumb and forefinger. "This is what you want. Not his blood."

"I shall take both," he said. "His blood *and* the ring."

She did not say a thing, but tipped her head back and placed the ring in her mouth. She smiled, grimaced, and swallowed.

"Now," she said, stepping halfway into the closest tunnel. "It is mine to keep. And while you strike him, I shall flee. All I need is a three-step lead to lose you in this maze."

Edwin dropped his arm in resignation. Brin relaxed. As did Rachel.

It was a mistake.

Edwin kicked Brin in the stomach and used that kick to push off toward Rachel. As Brin fell, clutching himself, Edwin dropped his sword, dove toward Rachel, and wrapped his arms around her waist.

Edwin threw her down. Her head hit the ground first, stunning her.

Before Brin or Rachel could react, Edwin spun back and grabbed his sword again. With his foot, he rolled Rachel toward Brin. Julius was still motionless to the side of them.

Edwin stood above Rachel and Brin, pointing his sword in their faces.

"Permit me to gloat," Edwin said. "I think such quickness is uncommon, is it not?"

Still on the ground, Brin put his arm around Rachel to protect her from Edwin.

Edwin laughed at his pitiful effort. "So your heart belongs to her, does it? What a shame I shall have to split her open to retrieve that ring."

Rachel shrank back into Brin's arms.

"Who wishes to die first?" Edwin asked. "Who wants to watch the other die?"

"You need not kill her to get what you need," Brin said.

"Certainly. I have no patience. I want the second ring now."

"I have what you need," Brin said. "Take it from me."

Surprise flickered across Edwin's face. "You had it all along? But I searched you. Twice. I shook out your clothes. Your shoes. Everything."

"I'm a gypsy," Brin said. "Always suspicious. I hid it the same way she did. Until nature took its course."

With slow, painful movements, Brin struggled to a sitting position. Because of the agony of his stomach, the effort nearly gagged him. Still on the ground, he leaned over, and removed his right shoe. He shook it, and a ring fell onto the floor. Brin tossed it up to Edwin.

"You have both rings," Brin said. "Take the jewels. Not our lives."

"I think not. It is much easier to slay you than go to the effort of tying you both while I search the crypt."

Edwin brought his sword up again.

"What if the crypt is empty of jewels?" Brin asked.

The huge broadsword wavered. "Impossible."

"Not if I entered here in the dead of last night and plundered it myself," Brin said. "I had one ring. Don't you think it would be child's play for a gypsy to steal the other from Julius and later return it while he lay sleeping?"

Edwin's eyes narrowed. "Then why come back today with these two?"

"Satisfaction," Brin said. "I thought Rachel had betrayed me. I wanted to watch the pain in her face as she and Julius walked into an empty crypt. They would never suspect me of the theft. Later, I intended to take the jewels at leisure from where I have them hidden."

Edwin drew a deep breath. He thought for several seconds. "No," he said. "You are lying. I will kill you both."

Brin smiled. "Then you shall never see those jewels. When I am dead, who will there be to tell you where they are hidden?"

Brin smiled again. "Forty large sacks of jewels, Edwin. Another 50 smaller sacks of silver and gold. It was no easy task to move them elsewhere in the catacombs. Out of the thousands and thousands of tombs, in the miles and miles of tunnel, where might they be?"

"You lie," Edwin said. Yet there was uncertainty in his voice.

"Hold the sword to my throat while Rachel opens the crypt," Brin said. "Then step inside and see for yourself. If I tell the truth, you give us our lives in exchange for the jewels. If I lie, then kill us both."

Silence. Deathly quiet silence.

"Stand," Edwin finally said. "Both of you."

They did, slowly. Edwin handed both rings to Rachel. Then he spun Brin around, gripped his shoulders from behind with one arm, and placed the blade of his sword against Brin's throat with the other.

"Open it," Edwin commanded coldly to Rachel. "One false step and I spill his blood."

27

Rachel stepped forward. She stood on her tiptoes to reach toward the slots high up on the wall. With a ring in each hand, she pressed them both into the slots at the same time.

There was the slightest of sounds, a light click that was heard only because the tunnel itself was so silent.

Then creaking.

It seemed the entire wall began to move. It slid inward, perfectly balanced on rolling balls. Had the situation not been so grave, it would have been a moment to marvel at the intricate and clever craftsmanship of the men who had labored on it centuries earlier.

The interior was dark.

"Stand where you are and hold the torch high," Brin said. "Give your brother a clear view of the emptiness inside."

Rachel took the torch and stood to the side of the opening. Yellow light flickered into the giant crypt. It was the size of a small room. The roof was arched, the inside filled with coffins.

From outside, still holding the sword to Brin's throat, Edwin spoke. "You said sacks of jewels. Yet I see coffins."

"I pulled the sacks from the coffins," Brin said. "Take me inside with you so that I cannot run away. Together we will find those coffins empty."

Edwin hesitated.

"I cannot run," Brin said. "Rachel will not flee and leave you to slit my throat. I want you to see them empty. To know I have moved them elsewhere. For Rachel and me, it is our only hope." Brin paused. "And your only hope of ever getting the jewels of St. Callixtus."

"We go forward," Edwin said. "Slowly. Remember, I carry the sword."

Brin shuffled forward, keeping his feet so close together his legs rubbed as he walked. He stepped through the exact center of the opening.

Edwin kept his grip on Brin's shoulders and followed.

Brin thought of the gypsy Marcel and the balancing act across the rope. It was a matter of perfect timing, of total concentration.

And Brin forced himself to relax, waiting for the single split second that he needed. Any earlier or any later than the one-half heartbeat of opportunity that was about to arrive and the sword blade against his throat would draw deep.

One step.

Two.

Three.

Then it came.

Edwin grunted a curse of startled pain and staggered sideways. With the quickness of hands that made him faster than any gypsy, Brin grabbed Edwin's wrist, pulling the deadly sword away from his throat.

For long, terrible moments, they were frozen like that. Both of Brin's hands braced against Edwin's strong wrist. Edwin straining to draw the sword inward. Brin could not push it any farther away. Edwin could not pull it closer.

Brin gritted his teeth with effort. His two arms against Edwin's one. The man was strong. His hot breath washed over Brin's neck.

"Die, gypsy," Edwin said. "Die."

How much longer could Brin hold the sword away?

Five seconds.

Ten. Fifteen. Twenty.

And then the sword began to bite into the skin of Brin's throat. Small lines of blood appeared.

Edwin grinned in cruel satisfaction.

Brin's arms began to collapse. He fell to his knees, gasping at the pain of nails piercing his skin.

"Die, gypsy," Edwin said, flexing his arms to cut through the cartilage of Brin's neck. "Die like the mongrel you are."

"Dear Jesus," Brin whispered. "I believe. Take me home."

To Brin, in his last moments of life, the tomb seemed to grow cold. His body tingled.

Suddenly and inexplicably, Edwin gasped in fear, looking beyond Brin.

Edwin dropped the sword.

"No!" he shouted in horror. "No!"

He fell to his knees and scrambled backward. "No!"

His last cry of horror was a strangled gasp, and he toppled sideways. Then he collapsed completely.

"Brin!" Rachel cried from the opening of the tomb. "Are you hurt?"

"Stay where you are!" he shouted to her without turning. He could not take his eyes off Edwin. He'd hoped and expected the bigger man would lose his strength, but he had not been prepared for the terror in Edwin's face when it happened. "Don't step inside! You'll be..."

It was too late. Rachel was already running toward him... then gasping with pain.

Brin slowly found his feet and turned to her.

"My feet," she said, stumbling as she neared him. "They have been pierced!"

Rachel fell in his arms. He held her. It had taken 15 or 20 seconds for Edwin to fall. Soon, she too would lose consciousness.

"I don't understand," she said, tilting her head to look in his eyes.

"Nails," Brin said. "Last night, I buried them upright just beneath the dirt. But I left a narrow path in the center to step through so I could be safe. It was a trap, meant for you and Julius. But I fell on them too."

Her words grew heavy. "The nails. Were they tipped with poison?"

"Lay your head on my shoulder," Brin answered. "I won't let you go."

"Am I going to die?" she asked.

"Yes," he said quietly.

"Oh, Brin, that makes me so sad. I have come to love you."

With one arm holding her, he used his other hand to stroke her hair as her eyes slowly closed.

"And I," he said, "have come to love you."

Her strength was fading, but she managed a sad smile. She tried to speak, but nothing came out.

Slowly, all of her movement ended.

For Brin too, the blurring darkness came. In his last moments of consciousness, Brin cradled her and set her down gently.

Then he let out a deep breath and fell beside her.

Angel Blog

Well, there you are.

A happy ending.

Some of you might disagree after watching Brin and Rachel collapse in the catacombs. But death is only a bad ending if it takes you away from our Father instead of to Him.

To me, the story has a happy ending because Brin had called out to our Father when he believed he would die. My duty with him ended then. He'd made the right choice, and as I heard him utter his last words to Rachel, I was already looking forward to welcoming Brin to the angel's side of existence and telling him about all the years I had watched over him.

But, as it turned out, he fooled me.

Because when I saw Brin next, it was still on your earth. Our Father permitted me one last visit with Brin, and for the first time in all the years I had spent looking over him, he and I actually had a conversation.

To be sure, it was only a brief conversation.

But I told him what was important.

The rest he'd find out on the other side, when all of us angels could rejoice at his arrival.

28

Alone, Brin reached the top of a high hill. The hill itself held only tall grass and the low, flat bushes of the Scottish moors. With no trees to impede his view, he saw the tops of other hills far away and lost in a gray mist that only added mystery to the sensations he already felt.

He began to cross the ridge, the wind blowing a wild sensation of freedom across his face and hair. His whole body trembled in anticipation.

His grandfather's kingdom would open up below him when he reached the opposite crest.

It did not take him long to reach the edge of the hill. He stepped forward and for the first time in his life saw it. A place he had never been, but somehow, a place his heart knew had always been waiting. No more would he wander through fields at night to pass away sleepless hours in his own solitary dance of darkness. No more would he feel the piercing pain of utter aloneness.

Deep in the valley below was a fortress rising high.

Brin wanted to shout with joy. Could it really be? *Home?* With his father's father, waiting for him with love?

Sun broke through the gray mist, as if an answer from heaven.

Brin took a deep breath. It had been a long time since tears rolled down his face. He dropped to his knees in a prayer of gratitude.

When he opened his eyes, a haggard old woman was standing in front of him.

Brin stood, startled.

"How did…" He looked in all directions. Here, in the tall grass, it was wide open. Surely he would have seen her approach. Had he spent that long in prayer?

"This kingdom will be yours someday," the old woman said. Her eyes glittered. She'd wrapped her head in dark rags as protection from the wind. "And I have a message for you. A promise."

Brin was still bewildered. Still looking around, as if trying to decide how the old woman had suddenly appeared in front of him.

"Who are you?" Brin asked.

The old woman squinted and looked in the distance, trying to decide whether to answer. Finally she gave him a strange smile. "An old friend."

"Old friend? But I've never seen you before."

"Listen carefully," the old woman said. "Follow the way of our Father in everything you do, and your kingdom will have peace and prosperity. Don't forget the poor. And treat all with justice."

"*Our* Father?" Brin echoed.

"Our Father," the old woman repeated. "The same one who sent me to protect you in the catacombs."

"You cannot know about the catacombs," Brin gasped. Only two others had been there with him. Rachel and Julius, and each had sworn the other to secrecy.

The old woman smiled a mysterious smile. "You think it was the potion on the nails that saved you. Haven't you ever wondered why Edwin died when it was only a sleeping potion you used? Why you and Rachel suffered no harm?"

"You cannot know about the hidden nails!" Brin protested.

"Edwin died of fright," the old woman continued. "He saw something behind you that no man can see and survive."

"Impossible!"

"Impossible? Nothing is impossible with our Father," the old woman said. She smiled again. "I should know. I was there."

"No!" Brin was truly afraid. How could this old woman know what had happened in the catacombs? How could she speak about it with such certainty?

"Our Father has a plan, Brin. And I got to be a part of that plan in your life."

Brin was silent.

"Goodbye," the old woman said. "Until I see you again on the other side."

"The other side?" Brin pleaded, shocked out of his silence. "Wait. You must tell me more."

Without warning, a hand touched his shoulder.

He whirled.

It was Rachel, who had come up the other side of the hill.

"Who are you talking to?" she asked.

"To…" Brin turned again to point to the old woman, but he saw only the tall grasses and the valley below.

He closed his eyes. What had just happened?

"You were speaking," she said. "But I saw no one."

Brin let out a deep breath. How could he explain his conversation with an old woman who appeared not to exist anymore?

"It's as beautiful as you promised during our months of travel," he said finally, sweeping his arms to indicate the valley. Later he would think more about what had just happened—and what it might mean. But now he would enjoy the first view of his long-awaited home…with his new wife.

"Forgive me for my mumbling," he said. "It was nothing."

She moved closer, letting him block the wind, wrapping her arms around his waist from behind him. She rested her chin on his shoulder to look down on the valley, thinking back on what had happened in the year since they had left Rome to travel by horse and boat back to England. Julius, nursed back to health. Secret arrangements with the Keepers of the Grail to use the incredible wealth of what St. Callixtus had left behind for good.

And—her chin on his shoulder as a reminder—Brin's sudden growth as he moved into full adulthood. He was close to four inches taller than her now.

"Forgiveness for your mumbling?" she echoed. "The only thing for which you'll never be forgiven is how you deceived me into declaring my love for you." She laughed.

"I did not lie to you in the catacombs," he said, slipping into their favorite argument. "For surely, unless the Lord returns, there will come a day when you die."

He was facing away from her, but she heard his grin as he continued the familiar ending to this argument, one she brought on as often as she could because she never tired hearing what he would say next.

"I pray, however, that day will not arrive until you are an old woman," he said. "And not until we have a brood of grand-children."

He paused as he always did. "After all, I am not to blame if the sleeping potion from your own bag of tricks took you before I could say what I needed to say."

"No, my dear beloved." She kissed the back of his neck lightly. "You are not to blame."

She stepped away from him and took his hand.

"Stay with me always," she said as she led Brin down the hill. "Your grandfather waits. And we have arrived where we belong."

Historical Note

Readers may find it of interest that the Catacombs of St. Callixtus indeed exist in Rome as described, were abandoned and forgotten as Julius described, and were not rediscovered until late in the fifteenth century.

Historical scholars still debate whether the Knights Templar were rightly or wrongly accused when their mighty order was dismantled by the rulers of France and England and Spain early in the fourteenth century.

No scholars have ever made mention of the Keepers of the Grail.

Sigmund Brouwer is a bestselling author whose novels include *The Last Disciple*, *The Weeping Chamber*, and *Out of the Shadows*. Among his books for children are the extremely popular Mars Diaries and the Accidental Detectives series. He, his wife, Cindy Morgan, and their two daughters live in Alberta, Canada.

Join the Supernatural Adventures of the Guardian Angel!

This guardian angel is working overtime in the lives of kids facing excitement—and danger—at every turn...

The Angel and the Ring

Brin, an orphaned, teenage gypsy, must learn to trust a mysterious girl and, ultimately, God to uncover the secrets of the one possession his parents left him—a ring.

The Angel and the Sword

When Raphael, a court jester, is falsely accused of attempting to murder the pope, his wits and his faith are all he has to solve the mystery in time to save his life and the lives of others.

The Angel and the Cross

When Marcellus, the son of a centurion of the Roman court, is kidnapped by Zealots and then rescued by a rebel's daughter, he is thrust into a quest for truth that will change history.